W9-CLO-746

let's do

BY REBECCA MEACHAM

2004 WINNER, KATHERINE ANNE PORTER PRIZE IN SHORT FICTION

University of North Texas Press
Denton, Texas

10 9 8 7 6 5 4 3 2 1

Permissions:
University of North Texas Press
P.O. Box 311336
Denton, TX 76203-1336

The paper used in this book meets the minimum requirements of the American National Standard for Permanence of Paper for Printed Library Materials, z39.48.1984. Binding materials have been chosen for durability.

Library of Congress Cataloging-in-Publication Data

Meacham, Rebecca, 1970-
  Let's do / by Rebecca Meacham.
      p. cm.
  "2004 Winner, Katherine Anne Porter Prize in Short Fiction."
  ISBN 1-57441-185-3 (pbk. : alk. paper)
  1. Middle West—Social life and customs—Fiction. I. Title.
  PS3613.E125L48 2004
  813'.6—dc22
                            2004014252

Let's Do is Number 3 in the Katherine Anne Porter Prize in Short Fiction Series

This is a work of fiction. Any resemblance to actual events or establishments or to persons living or dead is unintentional.

Slightly different versions of these stories have appeared in the following publications: "Trim & Notions" and "Let's Do" in *Indiana Review*; "Simple As That" in *The Journal*; "Good Fences" in *Michigan Quarterly Review*; "Worship for Shut-Ins" in *West Branch*; "Weights and Measures" in *Chelsea*; "Tom and Georgia Come Over to Swim" in *Beloit Fiction Journal*.

Cover image: Sherry Karver, "Off Broadway: Faces in the Crowd III" (2001), photo-based oil painting. Reproduced courtesy of Lisa Harris Gallery, Seattle, Washington.

Text design by Carol Sawyer/Rose Design

contents

acknowledgments

F or their encouragement, wit, and love, I thank my mother, Ruth Meacham, and my father, David Meacham. I am grateful for the kindness of my stepmother, Kay Meacham, and the endless generosity of the Duemey, Meacham, Rybak, and Santomauro families.

For sharing their stories and laughter, I thank my friends: Kelly Wilson, Allison Redmon, Jaymi Shroder, Michelle Barr O'Connor, Amy Brenner Cox, Christine Williams, Nicole Howard, Katie Lloyd, the women of Whitehouse, and countless comrades from McMicken Hall. I am grateful for the support and irreverence of my colleagues at UW-Green Bay, who have made Wisconsin a warm and wonderful place. Many thanks to the writers who have influenced this collection, especially Vivé Griffith, Jenn Gibbs, Cynthia Nitz-Ris, Alli Hammond, Julie Parham,

Francis Janosco, and Chip Gambill, all of whom, in one way or another, brought me sandwiches when I was hungry.

For their insight and all-around brilliance, I thank Brock Clarke, Erin McGraw, Tom LeClair, Amy Elder, and my mentors at University of Cincinnati and Bowling Green State University. I am deeply grateful to the editors who have given these stories homes, especially Danit Brown, and to the folks at University of North Texas Press, especially Karen DeVinney. Thanks to Jonis Agee and Barbara Rodman for reading and welcoming this collection. Special thanks to the Taft Foundation at the University of Cincinnati, whose support made this book possible.

Finally, I thank my lucky stars for the love my husband, Chuck Rybak, has brought into my life, and all the ways he has built a quiet place for me to write.

trim & notions

All afternoon, I've watched boy after boy impersonate middle-aged gamblers. I'm helping my friends Alan and Geneva cast the Valley County High School musical. Alan teaches English literature and Geneva teaches choir, while I'm a K-through-6 art teacher next door at County Elementary. Alan wants us to write evaluations in forms on our clipboards—he brought clipboards—and we're supposed to comment on each student's stage presence, appearance, vocal clarity, and so forth. It seems fussy to me, but the County High Spring musical is a pretty big deal. Everyone, especially the parents, goes a little nuts. The last director was fired for putting on *The Fantasticks*, which sounded like a superlative choice, until rehearsals got under way. The show turned out to be some stripped-down, avant-garde production—no splashy backdrops, no hot dance interludes, no sweeping chorus numbers. The parents fumed that their kids were denied their one shot all year to belt their guts out in wigs and boater hats. But they had a point, Alan admitted. "There were just nine characters in the show," he told me. "And one of them was a mute."

So this year, it's back to crowd-pleasers, which is why Alan chose *Guys and Dolls*. Besides Geneva and me, two other people are helping with auditions—reps from the parents' association, here to protect their children's interests. Bob and Mary are their names, I think, or something equally upstanding. They're both wearing patterned turtlenecks, one with strawberries, the other golf clubs. I'm nervous sitting next to them, since I'm sort of a scandal myself these days. It turns out that the last director left more than greasepaint in his wake. My baby boy is due in May, and I'm beginning to show under my smocks. The director ran off to Moab, Utah, to photograph the hoodoos. Which makes sense to me. He was the kind of guy you'd imagine would work best with giant rocks.

But that's all over now and only Geneva and Alan know about my situation. Otherwise, I've kept it pretty quiet. Or tried to. I haven't told my family, which technically is just two more people: my mother, who lives hundreds of miles away, and my older sister, Anne, from Albuquerque, who wants to visit in March. That gives me about a month to clean my house and come up with a way to tell her. Anne's been trying to nail down a man and begin breeding for many, many years. Plus, she tends to think I'm the spoiled one, the goody-goody who lands all the jobs and men, even if some don't stick.

Right now, landing our male leads seems completely hope-less. We have them working in pairs on the stage as we sit at a table. Two dweeby freshmen walk in and shake our hands, every one of us in a row, then plod through their lines. "Eensy," I write on my evaluation form. "Like cartoon mice." The next two boys wear their jeans so low on their bodies that I can't concentrate.

They're gesticulating like crazy and peppering the script with words like "Yo, Muthafucka!" and I keep worrying that their pants will fall down. "Boys," Alan interrupts them. "These characters are *gamblers*. Not gangstas. Can you cut the hip-hop crap?" The next pair thinks they're comedians. When Alan gives them the improv assignment—"Pretend you're a teacher at a school for tough guys. You're lecturing your students on how to talk, walk, act. Go with it"—they hear only "teacher" and launch into imitations of Alan, stuttering slightly over their "t"s and talking about phallic symbols. "Don't quit your day jobs," I write on the form, though I'm blushing on Alan's behalf. Phallic readings are his shtick. "It's the only way," he says, "you can get high school juniors to care one whit about Shakespeare."

Meanwhile, Bob and Mary clear their throats like decent people do when they hear a dirty joke. Geneva is trying not to laugh, and Alan is sort of smiling. He's somewhere between honored, mortified, and flunking them forever. He runs a hand through his floppy blond hair and readjusts his glasses. "That's enough, Chad and David," he says. "T-terrific work."

All I write for the next five pairs is "No" in different languages. By evening, it's clear we're getting dispirited. No boy in County High has the height or verve of Sky Masterson, the broad charm of Nicely-Nicely Johnson. When we finish for the day, I see that Geneva has forgone evaluations altogether. On her form is an impressive rendering of Snoopy on his doghouse. A balloon above his head says, "Yo. This Sucks."

When I get home, my sister has left a giddy message with precise instructions about calling her back. It's hard to tell whether she's excited or normal since Anne always sounds happy, or as some say, flaky. She's into sun signs and star charts and feng shui and tarot cards—any boost from the spiritual, she says, to smooth the earthly path. But I know that her mellow act is all a bunch of fizz; deep down, she's still the same bitter Anne who accused me of cheating whenever I won at Scrabble or outscored her SATs. Now she makes a modest living as an interior designer. A designer who wallpapers bedrooms in twigs and leaves for dippy New Age housewives, but it's a job, her first steady job, and this makes our mother happy. You learn to live with the lamps she makes out of deer skulls and junkyard wire. And for the most part, I admire Anne. They say Picasso looked at rusty handlebars and a bicycle seat thrown together in the trash and saw the head of a bull. My sister and I are scrappers, too, like crows, finding the shiny things in garbage. Not that stapling moss to a wall makes you a Picasso. Or that finding a shiny thing means it's anything worth keeping.

I take my vitamins and heat up some creamed corn—it's all I want to eat these days—and thumb through my mail. No letters. Nothing but promotions for tempera paint. I let my cat, Buzz Aldrin, inside and toss him a toy mousie. Buzz Aldrin has been pretty good company since the director moved out and, apparently, forgot how to use a pen. I dial my sister's number.

"So, I've found the One," my sister says, right when she answers the phone.

We've had this conversation at least thirty times. It does no good to remind her of the last One, who never brushed his teeth, or the One who could sleep only on satin sheets, or the One who received secret messages in songs by Michael Jackson.

"Uh-huh," I say. "What's this One's name?"

"Now Samantha," she chides. "I know you haven't had much luck with men lately, but be happy for your sister."

She can talk in a way that's both bubbly and biting, like hydrochloric acid. I should never have called her when the director left without so much as a forwarding address. I dread what she'll say when she sees me now, what weird pity she'll inflict.

"Okay," I sigh. "I'm interested. Where did you meet him?"

"On a rafting trip. He was a friend of the river guide. He has very sexy forearms."

"Name?"

"John Calloway."

This sounds too tame to be true. My sister gravitates towards men named Solarfire or The Dude.

"Hair?" I ask.

"Brown," she says.

"All of it?"

"It's all brown, yes."

"I mean, does he have all of it?"

"Yes, yes, he has all of his hair," Anne says. "It's curly. It's cute."

"Teeth?" I ask.

"Straight," she says.

"All of them?"

She waits for the rest.

"I mean, does he have all of them?"

"He's really great, Sam," she says. "He restores houses."

"That's a job?"

"Sure. He buys ramshackle old houses and fixes them up. Then he sells them again for lots of money. It's very lucrative."

I stifle a laugh. My sister, using the word lucrative. There has to be a catch. I ask, "His career doesn't concern you?"

"I'm not seeing your point."

"How do you know he won't make you a project, then unload you for the next dumpy thing?"

"That's not going to happen," she asserts. "Besides, how could you refuse a man who sees beauty in the rubble?"

"You're gushing," I say. "You're quoting some poet now."

"Oh, Sam," she sighs. "Don't you remember anything about romance?"

I look at my stomach. He's moving like crazy in there, cartwheeling I think. Sometimes when I'm completely still, I see something poking, an elbow maybe, maybe a heel. "I remember," I tell her. I rub my belly and he settles down. I imagine his eyelids, if he has them yet, fluttering, blinking, closing.

"Well, I want you to meet John," Anne says. "He's coming with me in March! You have all sorts of space now, right?"

I don't know how to answer. I was turning the spare room into my baby's nursery until I got so tired all the time. Everything is half-painted—the walls are the color of lemon meringue, and I'm thinking of putting clouds on the ceiling, since I've already made the stencils—it's really lovely and peaceful and gender-neutral, or will be when it's done.

"Um, sure," I say, wondering where I'll find the energy. Anne and John. *Guys and Dolls.* On top of teaching, painting, cleaning, shopping. My baby gives a mighty kick. I know, I tell him, I deserve it.

"Great!" Anne says. "We're driving and making a whole trip of it. John's thinking about bringing his dog. But he doesn't chew furniture or pee where he shouldn't—he's really good in the house."

"John is?"

"Sam! You are so funny! I can't wait for you to meet him!"

Since she never asks about me, we say goodbye pretty fast. I look around at the mess of my home, think of my poor cat fleeing from some uninvited Labrador, and consider crying, but I'm too tired. Meanwhile, Buzz Aldrin has chewed off the mousie's tail. He's holding it close and licking its ears in an unnerving sort of ecstasy. I feel for both of them.

Just when you think things can't get worse, an old lady will accost you and talk about her vagina.

It's Friday, a week after we finally cast the musical, which ended up fine once Alan did a sly bit of recruiting. It's amazing who will crawl out of the woodwork when you offer free absences in English to every senior who participates in the production. We had lines out the door for auditions, and I have the largest stage crew ever assembled to help me with sets and costumes. Now, I'm walking down the hall to my room, the Studio, which is actually a nice little isolated pair of rooms in the basement, where I hold class. Since I only see the other teachers when they drop off their students, I had managed to keep my situation quiet for a pretty long time. Which wasn't hard. The director was such a lost puppy when I found him—the parents' association was readying the rails—that everything we did had to be covert. We made up ridiculous disguises just for driving around, dressing him as an old lady or Italian barber or British dog show handler. He liked to improvise, in every department, which is how I got in this predicament. In general, I'm the type who sharpens the crayons and caps the glue—I sketch before I paint. As a kid, I prided myself on my erasers, how long I could keep them clean.

Sure, once school started, I could feel the other teachers' eyes on my stomach, and I got a few peripheral questions from Leticia Simmons, who teaches third grade and chain-smokes in her car when her kids are in my class. But until it was obvious, which it is now, everyone was delicate and sympathetic and kept their distance, whispering theories among themselves. I made sure no one knew about the director and me, so they all assumed I was abandoned by some mystery man over the summer. Which is pretty much true, so why embellish. I'm sure their versions are a whole lot more interesting than, "I woke up. There was a note with a smiley face and a 'Thanks for Everything—' on his pillow." No wonder this guy liked mutes.

Anyway, the only drawback to my studio is that it's next to the lunchroom, and pregnancy wreaks havoc with your sense of smell. Everything is amplified. On Thursdays, it's fish sticks and grilled cheese sandwiches, so during my planning hours I head to the library to eat and surf the Internet for set-design ideas. This is where Carol Vonderbrink finds me.

"Samantha," she says, smiling widely, closing in for a hug. She's always pulling people into her huge, pillowy bosom. She's a sweet, apple-faced, twinkly-eyed woman who teaches second grade reading. Unfortunately, she goes heavy on the rose perfume, which gives me a headache. So there I am, with a nose full of cafeteria cheese and processed fish and now, bottled roses from the drugstore, contemplating exactly how to set the Hot Box scenes—like the Cotton Club, or seedier?—and whether to paint hot air balloons on my baby's ceiling before my sister arrives. In other words, I'm feeling a little light-headed when Carol starts in.

"You're glowing these days," Carol says. "How are you feeling?"

This is the first time that anyone has head-on addressed my pregnancy, and to be honest, I'm relieved. I'm tired of avoiding the elephant in the room—the one in my stomach—so I unburden myself a little. "I tell you, it's been tough, Carol. I'm alone, you know. But I'm really excited, too."

"Yes," she says. "It must be hard to be alone through this. Do you feel comfortable . . . talking about the father?"

I like Carol, so I decide to give her a little something to take back to the whisperers, which is where this will all end up anyway. "Well, I'm not supposed talk about the father anymore." I drop my voice and make a show of looking around for eavesdroppers. "Since he was deported."

Carol's eyebrows peak, and she says, "Oh."

"It was all quite a shock."

She gasps and reaches for me again, so I hold my breath and go with it. "These foreigners!" she moans. I nod against her shoulder.

Then, she brightens and says, "I notice your ankles are pretty swollen," which I hadn't really realized. Except for my monthly check-ups, my routine and wardrobe have stayed pretty much the same. I've been wearing my usual jumpers and smocks and cruddy old wool clogs. Now I see that my legs look like fire hydrants shoved into baby shoes.

"I guess they are."

"You know, when I was carrying my Bill and my Nancy, I had an enormous amount of discharge." She shakes her head. Her sleek silver bob bounces in emphasis.

"Well," I say.

"I had to wear sanitary pads throughout the second trimester."

"Gosh," I say.

"How's your discharge?" she asks, in that perky teacher's voice.

This is not exactly a discussion I planned to have with Carol Vonderbrink. I'm trying to reconcile excessive discharge with this sweet old woman who reads aloud from *The Adventures of Squirrel and Nut*, when she says:

"And then, once they were born, my vagina got very rubbery."

"Rubbery—?"

"Like those dishwashing gloves." Carol sighs. "It was really never the same."

I stand up. I start collecting my things to leave, but my center of gravity is off, so I sit down hard on the floor. Carol cries, "Oh!" and kneels and frets, pulling me to her chest. "Are you all right, dear?" The librarian and two parent helpers rush over in a swirl of perfume and concern. After a good deal of talk about blood sugar and blood pressure and fainting and emergency rooms, I negotiate my release. They help me stand and support my elbows as I walk to the door. I make my way to the hallway and step outside, breathing the crisp air, hoping my baby will be okay, apologizing for the scare. I promise him things will get better after lunch.

Instead, my afternoon becomes a parade of wombs and stretch marks and popping belly buttons, as teacher after teacher addresses my stomach. While the students diligently cut colored tissue for a stained-glass window project, out in the hallway their teachers recount heart-stopping stories of gestation and labor. Beth Simmons' nipples grew big as salami slices and never returned to size; Helen James' sister got ripped up in delivery, creating what Helen calls "a vaganus." Jenny Chang delivered caesarean but they put her bladder back in wrong. On a lighter note, Mary Lester's son was misidentified by several ultrasounds as a girl. "We had everything monogrammed, too," she laughs, "all these adorable pink fluffy dresses. But when he came out, there it was, no doubt whatsoever. A boy." Then, with obvious pride, she says, "I mean, I don't know how they missed his diddle, because it's awfully honkin' big."

After school, it's a relief to go next door and see Alan and Geneva, the only two people in Valley County Schools who haven't been pregnant, and whose insides I can't even begin to imagine. We're all heading to the arts supply warehouse to gather stuff for the *Guys and Dolls* sets and costumes. Geneva's choir room is decorated in life-sized photos from Mozart's *The Magic Flute*—heavily powdered actors in wildly colorful bird costumes. So it's relaxing to sit there in relative peace while she berates her altos for numerous offenses. "Slack-asses," she grumbles when they leave. "Chewing up Latin like it's Juicyfruit. And why bother with tempo or pitch? Like, you know, cause Britney doesn't." She twists her long, candy-red hair into a knot and stabs a pencil through it. She looks at me. "So how was your day?"

"Carol Vonderbrink has a rubbery vagina," I say.

She laughs heartily. "Oh, honey, that's such old news."

Geneva is large and theatrical and I'm thin, usually, and wimpy-looking, which makes Alan say, whenever he sees us, "If it isn't Mutt and Jeff." Which I've never understood. But as we walk through his door today, he's deep in conversation with Bob and Mary, who are now weighing in on all aspects of the musical, including set design and costumes. As we all pile into a school van and head over to the art warehouse, it's clear Alan's having a hard time. Apparently, Bob and Mary are troubled by the bawdier aspects of the show. This includes everything that has to do with Dolls.

"Look, the girls perform at the 'The Hot Box.' That is what it's called. It's a nightclub. It's sensual. It's supposed to have lewd overtones," Alan says, pulling into the warehouse parking lot.

Next to me, in the backseat, Mary asks, "But is it absolutely necessary to use the word 'Box'?" Today she's wearing plaid wool pants and a kitty-cat pin on her pea coat. "It's such a nasty word to use around children."

"Right," says Bob, who's wearing, of all things, pink chinos. "Why not call it 'The Hot Club,' or 'The Hot Bar'?"

Geneva and I escape the van, and she whispers in my ear, "Why mince words? Let's just call it 'The Hot Twat.'"

"Or 'Carol's Rubber Room.'" We giggle like juvenile delinquents on a field trip and leave Alan to fend for himself.

The arts supply warehouse always makes me giddy. It's the art-teacher equivalent of a candy store, but better, because everything is weird and new and, most importantly, free. The warehouse is a giant receptacle for the odds and ends of industry—the errors and the overproduced—like dented sheets of corrugated tin or boxloads of surplus shoelaces. I come here once a year or so to collect things for my classes. We wheel our cart past barrels of shiny buttons you scoop out with a sandbox shovel, barrels of plastic Easter eggs, barrels of broken seashells the size and shape of toenails, barrels of yarn from bad dye-lots, too marbled or ugly to sell. Racks of nicked CDs bounce rainbows in the light. Bolts of velvet, organza, silk, and fishnet vamp and wave as we breeze by. Geneva plucks a huge clam-shaped rattan purse from a heap marked "Damaged-Out." I stop the cart at a stack of designer interior paint, piling in cans of charcoal, coffee, buttercream, and robin's egg for the street sets: pavement, buildings, sky.

We pull around to Trim & Notions, my favorite aisle, if only for the name, which sounds dirty and prim at the same time, like Victorian pornography. Here, we sort through boxes of feathers and bright cloth peonies intended, it seems, for hats. I'm trying to remember the design of the Hot Box dancers' costumes in the movie. The flowers look a little water-damaged and smell faintly like smoke.

"Factory fire," says a man behind us. He's about my age, maybe younger, and wearing a warehouse smock and softly faded jeans. I try not to notice how nice his thighs look or wonder about anything else in there, since what's the point now, anyway. Geneva pinches my elbow. She doesn't like men, or women, really, except maybe herself.

"Those are from a milliner's business," the man says. His voice is deep and slightly accented. He has thick, pepper-colored hair that cries out to be combed by a woman's fingers. I lean forward on the cart and let the folds of my coat hang loose over my stomach.

"What happened?" I ask, stupidly.

"He said there was a fire," whispers Geneva. "Work with us here."

His eyes are the color of pennies. "Actually, there is a story," he says. "Rumor is that the factory owner set the fire. Hat business sinking, big insurance policy. And then he gets to write off all the damaged goods." He takes a giant peacock feather and raises it, like a question.

"Shrewd," I say. For the first time in months, I wonder what my hair looks like.

From the next aisle, I can hear Alan insisting to Bob and Mary that, politics or no politics, the Havana scenes must be set in Cuba. Geneva rolls her eyes and says, "I'll run interference." She strolls away and loudly asks Alan what we should do for palm trees. The warehouse man and I look at each other. I smile and he smiles back.

"Too many cooks," I say. "We're doing a high school musical. *Guys and Dolls.*"

"A-ha," he says. "It is always complicated. Have you seen these? They just arrived." He grabs a box from a shelf above me. In it are slender green and red ribbons, coiled like apple peels.

"What are they?" I ask.

"Bra straps. Surplus from Victoria's Secret."

Our hair almost touches as we look into the box. His breath smells like spearmint. Around his throat is a blue clay bead on a leather string. On closer look, it turns out his eyes are flecked with bits of gray.

I have no idea what to do with red and green bra straps. "I'll take fifty," I say.

Together, Stefan—we introduce ourselves—and I count them out. To be sure, I have him recount them. Then it occurs to me that the Hot Box costumes require around 100 feathers. Not to mention 100 peonies. Standing there, counting and laughing and heaping whimsy like treasure, it's like we're in our own enchanted corner. Stefan bunches a dozen feathers and offers them like a bouquet. I get silly and tuck a flower behind my ear. The day's weirdness and noise and bruising candor all but disappear.

When we're finished, my cart is full, so Stefan offers to get me another. But as I wait for him, still leaning on the cart to hide myself, my back begins aching as usual. My baby somersaults and I contemplate my fat, idiotic ankles. I remember all the foolishness that got me here in the first place. What am I doing? Pregnant and flirting with some warehouse stock boy, a foreigner, no less. Carol Vonderbrink would shake her silvery head. Any minute, Bob and Mary might wheel up and scold me, in those pants. Anne would get a good laugh, too, since she's so together now—her perfect little sister, so straight and narrow, trolling the junkstore aisles for any remainder with a pulse and kindly smile. And then I hear something cutting the director said before he vanished: *Why do you always care so much what other people think?*

I hightail it out of there and find Alan and Geneva, who are giving Bob and Mary a task. "We need brass buttons for the Salvation Army costumes," Geneva says, pointing them towards a barrel full of buttons in every conceivable metal. She hands them a pie plate to fill. "*Only* brass." We walk away. Somewhere at the other end of the warehouse, a Frenchman is wheeling an empty cart in search of an unwed mother. Oh, well. Probably happens every day. Right now, we have the chance to do some work. We stroll the aisles. For awhile, we lose ourselves among sheet metal, plywood, cracked flowerpots, curtain fringe, and clapperless bells—at home with the dents and scraps.

If I don't tell her, my sister will, so the day before Anne comes into town, I decide to call my mother. She lives in a retirement community in Florida. Before that, she lived in this house and worked as a secretary for thirty years. She taught us to be meticulous, organized, and plan everything in life, which turns out to be harder than I thought, which is why I've been putting off calling her. My sister and I get our artistic side from her. After Dad died when we were little, Mom took in sewing for extra cash. But her real skill lies in fashioning charm from disaster, like painting smiley faces in iodine on your bloody scraped knees, or patching your jeans with crackled suede—as seen on all the supermodels— right before your big date. And until now, I've been pretty good at leaving all the disasters to Anne. I met my only other boyfriend, Ned, as a college freshman and thought we'd get married, until last year. Mild, kind, accountant Ned who left me for a man in a chat room. Which turned out to be a good thing, since I'd been trying to end it or get engaged for several sexless years.

There's talking and splashing in the background as they hand my mom the phone, so I'm guessing she's playing cards by the pool. I can picture her wearing Jackie-O sunglasses, smoking as she bids trump.

"Samantha, sweetie! What's going on? Is your sister in trouble again?"

"Anne is fine, Mom. She's coming to visit. She's bringing some new guy."

"Oh, dear. Better hide your jewelry."

I tell her what I know about my sister's new man and how I'm working on the musical and general updates about my students. Then I mention I'm painting the house, specifically mine and Anne's old room.

"Really, sweetie. How are you doing it? I always wanted to do pink."

"Actually," I say, "I'm thinking of doing it in clouds."

"Mmm," Mom says, then under her breath, "Three clubs."

"And maybe some hot air balloons. With little lambs riding in the baskets."

This gets her attention. "Hot air balloons and what, sweetie? That sounds eccentric."

"It's for the baby." My heart is beating out of my chest.

"What baby? Is your sister in trouble again?"

"No, Mom, I told you. Anne is fine."

"Because you're too stable and grounded and orderly about things . . ."

I take a deep breath. "It's my baby. It's a boy. I'm at twenty-nine weeks."

On the other end of the phone, she's so quiet I can hear the other ladies making bids.

"Mom?"

She makes a funny whooping sound I've never heard before. "A grandbaby! I'm having a grandbaby! My daughter's having a little boy!" For the next few minutes, she announces this to everyone at the pool. There seems to be lots of cheering.

When she talks to me again, she says, "Well, it's about time."

"You're not mad?"

"Well it would have been nice to know sometime during the last six months that we've talked on the phone."

"You're supposed to tell me that I know better and I should have been more careful and now I've ruined our good name."

"Ah, Samantha, you should hear some of the stories around here. Florence Dussledorf's sons have made six grandbabies for her, all by different mothers. She never gets to see them. Everyday it breaks her heart. And Bertie Highsmith, her stepdaughter used a surrogate who ended up keeping her grandbaby. Oh, and Myrtle West has that lesbian daughter who—"

"So you're okay with it?"

"I'm fine. What about the father?" Mom asks.

"It's that director guy I tried to rescue over the summer. But he's skipped town. He doesn't know."

"Good. He was too quiet, anyway. Faded right into the wallpaper."

"You never met him, Mom."

"A mother knows these things. And so will you, soon enough. Oh! I'll have to dust off those crochet needles! Your little boy will need a blankie!"

We talk for awhile about how big I am and how big she got
with Anne and me. Since she only half-listens to health news and
invents the rest, she offers lots of strange advice, which along with
all the other information I've been getting lately, makes me even
more worried. "Well, if you get too nervous," she says, "make
sure you drink vodka or you'll go into early labor." At the same
time, she believes in the pyrotechnic power of the body. "You
shouldn't eat anything with vinegar," she warns. "It can make your
stomach explode." Stomach exploding has always been a big
thing with her. Cherry pits, baking soda, expired eggs, rock
candy—all of these are ticking bombs. On the other end of the
spectrum is my sister, who believes internal organs have con-
sciousness, possibly intelligence. "Don't you feel sorry for your
liver?" Anne will ask, just out of the blue, and then go on to
explain how hard the liver labors for us, endlessly filtering wine
and aspirin and hormones in dairy foods and cocaine and pesti-
cides, and all for what? Is anyone ever grateful?

Mom tells me to forget painting the baby's room if I have to
climb up ladders, which I wouldn't dream of now, anyway. "I fell
once when I was carrying Anne," she says. "It scared the wits out
of your Daddy, God rest his soul. Oh, your Daddy would be so
happy for you, Samantha. He'd give you such a hug." She sighs.
"Right after he hunted down and killed your baby's no-good
absent father."

Dad flew jets for the Air Force and was a starch and polish
kind of guy, so I wonder if he really would be happy for me, or
just confused and disappointed. Either way, it makes me sad.
Mom wishes me good luck in dealing with my sister, and hangs
up with promises of booties.

On Sunday, a giant SUV pulls into my driveway and my sister comes running out. She's decked out in full jingly regalia—long flowy skirt, beaded blouse, patchwork coat with toggle buttons. Anne isn't much for zippers. Her hair is long and frizzy and grayer than the last time I saw her, but her skin is flawless. You'd never believe she's thirty-five and spends a lot of time playing with antlers.

I stand on the porch, shivering a little, since there's still snow dotting the ground. I'm wearing a thin knit dress that hugs my belly like a net around a basketball.

Anne stops dead in her tracks when she sees me. Her eyebrows arch. "Something's different about you, I just know it," she says, staring at my middle. "Did you cut your hair?"

"Hey, big sister," I say, laughing. "I guess I have some news."

"I'll say you do," she says. She hugs me as best she can, then pats my belly. "Always have to be the first at everything, don't you."

A man's voice calls Anne from the truck. John opens his door. He's tan and tall and gray at the temples, wearing a collared shirt tucked into his jeans. He appears to be showered and shaved, which throws me. Anne's never dated a man with a haircut.

"Samantha, I take it?" He strides up and shakes my hand— firm grip, nice calluses. He smells fresh, like pine needles. He has good presence and wonderful vocal clarity. Leading man material.

"Congratulations," he says, smiling. "Anne didn't tell me you were expecting."

"I think we're all surprised," Anne says in that bright, mean voice.

"How was the trip?" I change the subject.

They both laugh and say, "Muddy." As they unload trampled-looking backpacks from the truck, they tell me about the weather and camping across the cold, wet Midwest. John is originally from Arizona, it seems, and Anne's forgotten how long it takes for spring to reach Indiana. "I made us stay in a hotel last night so we'd be presentable for you," she says, and he says, "*Made* us? It's more like you finally let us!" But for all the dirt and surprises and exhaustion, they seem happy, like they've conquered something together.

"It was actually quite nice," Anne says, loosening up. "The trees were budding, and the browns and grays everywhere gave me some ideas for my next bedroom."

Typical Anne. She gets thrown a curve but rides it out, even makes it pretty. Something ripples through my chest. At first I think it's heartburn or the baby kicking, but as I watch them pulling off their boots and tapping the muck off and arranging them side by side on the porch, I know it's not a pregnancy thing. The feeling is older and more familiar, like when you swallow something sharp and it takes forever to absorb.

The truck starts barking. John says, "That's my cue," and pulls some tennis shoes from his backpack. "Sam, how do you feel about dogs?"

"I'm fine," I say, "but Buzz Aldrin might freak out."

He looks at me like everyone does when I mention the name of my cat. "My tabby. A stray. He fell onto my roof from I don't know where and decided to adopt me."

"So he's the cat from outer space," John says.

"Like the movie!" Anne says. "Remember, Sam? We loved that movie."

What I remember is Anne telling me, when the theater went dark, that a man with a taste for children's ankles lived under the seats. "Does your dog like cats?" I ask.

"Especially with ketchup, ba dum bum," John says.

I say, "Don't quit your day job."

The dog, Murphy, bounds out of the car and pees on my lawn for about a half an hour. Which, since my bladder is now an ottoman, I completely understand. The dog takes a few laps around the yard and then all three of them come inside to sniff around my living room. Buzz Aldrin runs for his life. Anne looks over everything to make sure I've displayed her crafts. "Where's the lampshade?" she asks, meaning the lampshade she made from dried leaves, which happen to smolder when heated.

We need to figure out sleeping arrangements so we tour the house, which hasn't really changed since Mom gave it to me years ago. Ned encouraged me to paint the kitchen a dramatic burgundy, which the director called a rather obvious metaphor for sexual repression. The director prided himself on being hard to interpret. He liked to arrange weird still-lifes, so here and there you'll find a cheap rubber ball on a silver tray, an antique bowl filled with dead bees. But walking through rooms now with John and Anne, who remake houses for a living, I'm struck by how much looks the same as when we were growing up—the dark wool slipcovers, the velvet curtains, mom's handiwork draped like funeral veils.

"God, was it always so dark in this place?" Anne asks. "All that's missing is a ghost."

But John is a good guest and admires the crossbeams, the hardwood floors and scrolled banister. We get to my and Anne's old room, which is in total disarray. "This must be the nursery," she says. "So why don't you tell me all about how I'm going to be an aunt?"

John says he'd love to take Murphy on a walk and give us a chance to catch up, so Anne gives him directions to the park. She keeps staring at my belly, sometimes laughing, sometimes shaking her head.

"Was it that stupid director guy?"

"Look, I feel dumb enough already," I say.

"I don't mean that you're stupid. I mean that he was a pretentious jerk."

"I know. I messed up across the board." I feel too heavy to keep standing, but there's no furniture in here yet. I lean against the wall and work my way to the carpet, fumbling to the floor with the grace of a cow break-dancing. Anne stares at me, uncomprehending, like I'm acting out charades. Then, she arranges herself into a neat lotus position.

"So I'm sure you told Mom already."

"Yesterday."

"Jesus, Sam. What's the rush? Why not wait and let your child tell everyone for you?"

"Well, what was I supposed to do? This isn't exactly my style."

"And what did Mom say?"

"She was happy. Really happy. She's thrilled to be a grandma."

Anne folds her arms and says in that Sam-always-get-the-bigger-slice voice, "Uh-huh. That figures." She looks at my belly with such intensity that I look at it, too. "So for the past eight months—when are you due?"

"End of May."

She's tapping her fingers on her arms, trying to work out the math. "So for . . . many months, you've been too *embarrassed* to tell your only sister about the biggest event in your life? In my life?"

"No, that isn't why. That's not it at all."

"What is it then?"

To be honest, I can't think of any other reason, so I pretend the baby's kicking. I make a face and rub my belly and say a little "Oooh."

But Anne doesn't bite. "I am going to be an aunt, for heaven's sake, and you don't tell me about it for half a year. I can't believe you, Samantha Jane. Are you really so ruled by shame?"

I look at the carpet, feeling puny, noticing the grit and paint mashed into the weave. It sounds so much worse when she puts it like that.

"And they call *me* self-centered," Anne says.

"What can I say, Anne? I'm really sorry. It's not like I've been enjoying this."

"And that's the other thing!" she shouts, slapping the floor. "You're having a baby. You have a job and a house and friends and a family. Why shouldn't you enjoy it? My god, if I were pregnant, I'd be dancing and singing like something out of Disney."

"You do that anyway."

"The point is, I wouldn't care. It's not a crime, Sam. It's not some black mark on your record. It's a baby."

"I know."

"I mean, Jesus, hooray! A whole other person! Your future!"

"I get it, Anne."

"It's totally different from here on out. A beautiful, endless, magical journey."

"*Okay.*"

"Every single thing in your life is going to change."

I swear, Anne can vault onto her high horse with the pomp of a circus act. "Well, aren't you the smart one these days," I say. "Tell me, have you had a baby? Or are you channeling some wisdom from the Great Earth Mother? Because last time I looked, I was the only one here actually growing a human being. I think I know what I'm getting into."

Her eyes narrow like she's going to pull my pigtails. Instead, she stands up. Looking down at me, she says, "No, Sam. I don't think you have any idea what you're getting into. You want everything neat and tidy." She points to the ceiling, where my cloud stencils are still taped up, some of them filled in. "Look at this. You've always painted by numbers. You can't do that anymore."

"Oh, go suck an antler," I say.

"It's true. You've never been able to freehand. You never leave anything to chance."

"Please! This, from the woman whose last boyfriend wrote a bad check to a prostitute!"

"I'm not ashamed of my past," she says. "I may not play it safe like you, but I don't hide. And I don't wallow."

"Right. You just post bail."

"You can't stand it when I'm right," she says, heading out the door. "Your fucked-up older sister actually knows how to deal with life. Imagine."

"Yeah! Imagine!" I wobble forward and reach over to slam the door to our old room, the thunder of ancient battles. Poor old door, probably thought it had retired. A stencil flutters down. I sit there on the cruddy carpet, staring up at a ceiling I've stared at my whole life, at the precise outlines of painted clouds, and wonder how I'm ever going to pull myself back up to stand.

Just when you think things can't get any worse, your fucked-up older sister announces she's engaged.

They tell me in the evening, when we're sitting down to a dinner John's made—of course he cooks—of corn chowder and some sort of homemade flatbread. As usual, Anne and I ignore this afternoon's events, Anne because she has to keep pretending she's responsible and nice, and me because I'm the host. With the smell of food, Buzz Aldrin ambles into the kitchen and, without drama, sniffs Murphy's nose, then shoves his face into the dog's ear. Anne looks at me with that see-how-easily-different-species-manage-to-get-along expression, but I continue talking only to John, who has by now told me everything there is to know about joists. Believe it or not, you can completely exhaust the topic of house frames if you have a few hours to kill.

When I miss the chance to fill a pause with yet another question, Anne says, "So, Samantha, we have some news of our own."

They tell me the story: A campground near the Meramec River. The ring falling in the mud. The frantic, giggly search. Then, of all things, they actually sing the rest of it: Down came the rain to wash the mud away. Then came the sun to dry up all the rain. And Anne and her fiancé got on the road again. They're very amused with themselves.

"I guess we had lots of free time in the car to get creative," John says. Anne gazes at him adoringly. She pulls a necklace out of her collar and the ring hangs from it: a traditional square cut white diamond, about a carat, plain gold band.

"Well, I always wondered how Anne would get engaged," I say. That familiar burning feeling wedges in my throat. "I guess I expected tattoos. Or a shotgun."

I'm dreading they'll start to sing again, so when the phone rings I'm so grateful, I practically hurdle the dog. It's Alan. "Bob and Mary are threatening to shut us down," he says. "They say there's too much gambling."

"Alan, this is not a good time," I say.

"So, I asked them, what did you think these characters did? Their names are Big Julie. Harry the Horse. Nathan Detroit. I mean, they were there at the auditions, right?"

There's no getting out of this. Across the kitchen, John clears the plates and Anne starts rinsing them, dishes passing between them in a quiet, comfortable rhythm. She flicks him with water from her hands. He laughs and pokes at her with a dirty fork.

"So finally," Alan is saying, "I told them they could have some authority over the music."

My other line beeps in and I put Alan on hold. "Has that weasel Alan called you yet?" Geneva shouts into my ear. "No wait, weasels have spines. What doesn't have a spine?"

At the sink, John walks up behind my sister and wraps his arms around her waist. He whispers in her ear and she laughs. He rests his hands across her flat little belly.

Geneva gives me an earful: Alan gave Bob and Mary control over the songs. Alan is a traitor. Alan is weak. Alan gave Bob and Mary control over the sets. Everywhere I look, wheels are falling off and bouncing willy nilly in the road.

I switch the line back to Alan. "Alan, tell me what's happening with the sets," I say as calmly as I can.

"Is that Geneva on the other line?"

"Tell me right this minute."

Alan sighs. "Sam, they wanted to make major character changes. Deep structural stuff. I threw them a bone."

"So you have me working on the buddy system?"

"They just want to be involved. And see all your sketches in advance. And approve the paint. Sam, it's only cosmetic. They have the kids' moral interests at heart."

My sister and John are swaying side to side. John twirls Anne around and her skirt fans out. She hitches her skirt dramatically. John claps his hands like a flamenco dancer. Much more of this nonsense and my belly button won't be the only thing to pop.

I work to keep my voice level. "Alan, this is a goddamn musical about gamblers who end up repenting their sins. In a goddamn chapel. There's even a song about it. Two white, heterosexual, middle-aged couples fall in love and end up getting married. There's even a song about that. Every goddamn thing ends up perfect for every goddamn one. And you're having a hard time making this *acceptable* for the goddamn kids?"

"Um, Sam, are you all hormonal or something? You're due pretty soon, right?" he asks. I hear a click as Geneva hangs up. "Oh wait, give me a minute," Alan says. "That's my other line."

I slam down the receiver and the phone rings again. "What the hell is it now?" I answer. Anne and John stop their little show and look at me, astonished.

"Samantha?" It's a man's voice, slightly accented. "Hello. This is Stefan. From the Art Warehouse. How are you doing this evening?"

"Good, good, I'm good," I lie.

"I hope I am not imposing."

"No. I'm just having a little dinner. With my sister. She's visiting." My mind is racing. I wonder what I must have dropped or spilled or broken. I wonder how he got my number. I wonder if I can go into labor simply by answering the phone.

"Oh. Sorry to interrupt. I wanted to let you know we have some more flowers from the milliner. Another factory, up in smoke. This guy has terrible luck."

"My goodness, yes, it's dreadful." I sound like my mother.

"But then I started thinking about that song, from your show, what is it, 'Luck be a Lady.' So I thought of you."

I wonder if he can hear me blushing. "I bet you say that to all the set designers." Anne and John just stand there, watching me like I'm television. I turn my back.

Stefan laughs. He asks me if I want to come in and pick up some more notions. Ha, I want to say, that's all I need, a few more crazy notions. Plus, there's no coat big enough now to cover everything up. Talk about terrible luck. So I tell him it's not such a good idea. Maybe Geneva can come in for me, or maybe Bob and Mary. My heart droops like a hundred wilted peonies.

"Oh. I'm sorry to hear you can't come in," Stefan says. "Is there a problem with your baby?"

I'm so surprised I can't speak. Either this guy is wonderful or some kind of wackjob. In any case, it figures I'd get more action when I'm knocked up than any other time. With Alan and Anne yelling at me all day, my brain is whirling like a roulette wheel, and I'm so dazed that I say No, everything's fine with my baby, it's very sweet of you to ask. Maybe when my sister leaves I'll get a chance to stop in. He tells me he would like that very much.

When the phone rings again and it's Carol Vonderbrink, I answer all her questions and even ask a few. The conversation grosses John and Anne out enough that they leave to cuddle on the couch. When Bob and Mary call about my sketches, I agree to meet them for lunch on Tuesday. When my mom calls with a list of her favorite names of leading men—Gary, Cary, Humphrey, Clark—I listen and even give the phone to Anne, so she can share her news. I toddle out to the couch and sit by my future brother-in-law, who in the end, seems like a stand-up guy. He asks if he can touch my belly. I say go for it. He reaches hesitantly, then plants his hand right at the equator.

"She's delirious with joy, Sam. This may be the best week of Mom's entire life," Anne says, walking in. "Oooh! Is he kicking?"

She sits next to me and places her hand under John's. They tell me they want to give their nephew a present—the nursery—they'll take care of everything. I can't imagine how any of this will come together, but I guess that's another thing you learn to live with. "Is there anywhere close we can get supplies?" Anne asks, and I say I know just the place. My sister wonders if the baby can dream yet, what a baby's dreams might look like. Which gets me thinking. I see the nursery walls awash in mud brown or spring green, blooming with tree buds or farm animals or whatever spirit guides Anne's brush. A sky full of stenciled clouds clears above our heads.

"Was that a kick?" John asks, though nothing's happened.

"Just hold on," I say. We're all quiet in that funny illogical way, like when Anne and I were little and we'd hold our breath at night, thinking if we lay still enough, we'd conjure shooting stars. We sit like that now, in the dark, and wait for the show to begin.

good fences

Bill's mailbox, an old country thing, flag-
armed and rusting, perches at the edge of his property across
from an abandoned red schoolhouse. His wife Lynn complains
that the mailbox is tacky; Bill tells her it's rustic. To make his
point, on the side of the box, he has stenciled their last name in
brown log-shaped letters. In the late afternoons, he sets out to
unlatch its tin door, walking a mile along the dirt drive that cuts
through the woods. During winter in the Ozarks, mail arrives just
before sunset unless snowfall or melt-off blocks the main road,
and some evenings Bill returns home empty-handed. But after
thirty-five years of quotas and company meetings, he is content to
wait for his *Forbes,* his wife's *House and Garden.* He has nothing
but time now, he tells his sons on the phone. In fact, he has time
now to name every tree on his land, to memorize the American
vice-presidents and read all of Shakespeare, to shoot holes in soda

can rows without worry—the nearest neighbor lives sixty acres away.

This afternoon on his way to the mailbox, Bill stops to whistle for Delia, his wife's toy collie, a lapdog with long, burr-catching hair. An impractical dog for a life in the woods, but Delia is good company, and Bill doesn't mind stopping every few yards to coax clumps of snow from her paws. Wind stirs the trees, snapping the ice-covered branches. Even in stillness, the woods crack and clamor; after two years, Bill is amazed by the racket. Packing up their home in Grand Rapids, he had listed for Lynn all the noises they'd leave: their young neighbors' stereos and all-night drunken barbecues, the sudden tear of a motorcycle down their street, the crunch and groan of nearby highway construction. Think of it, he had told her: the doorbell will never ring as you step in the bathtub. He had been trying to convince her that some losses were good, like the job that no longer kept him on the road. But he had been wrong—the middle of nowhere was surprisingly loud. In the summer, whippoorwills and frogs chirp until dawn, and throughout fall, turkey vultures rustle in the trees. At night, the sounds become minor chords. Sometimes, distant howls draw him to the porch, where he sits with his new twenty-gauge propped nearby, just in case. Once, a sad mewing rose from the woods and he readied his flashlight, until he heard something else—something heavier than Bill—thrash through the thicket and drag the mewing away. Then everything fell silent, held like a breath.

The land claimed whatever you didn't claim first—Bill realized this soon after they moved. In those early months, Lynn shuddered at the tarpaper houses along the main road, yards littered with ovens and skeletoned cars. To make her laugh, he recalled Dog-patch and twanged the theme song from *Deliverance*, but he was grateful that they never saw anyone in the flesh, no one sitting on porches or gathering clothes from the lines. Since they could stay in their house for months on end (if they wanted), it seemed like the elements, as Lynn called them, could be kept at bay. And at first, it was sort of charming when field mice nested in the car engine. Then Bill found a half-empty Pabst can on their boat dock. In the paper some days, he reads of moonshine-drunk men staggering off cliffs by the lake, shooting brothers-in-law, stealing boats off hitches. Some nights Delia barks at things he can't see—things, he is certain, that can easily see him as he stands aglow in the bay window, peering out in the darkness. So last spring, he wired a new alarm system through the gate. His gadgety brother from Nebraska arrived with a security camera, which they anchored in plain sight above their porch door. As he walks, a little faster now as the light starts to fade, the drive rises and snakes through trees posted with "No Trespassing" signs, each warning hammered by Bill himself.

He stops at the mailbox and orders Delia to sit. As he heaps his wife's catalogs into his arms, Delia growls. He turns slowly. Across the road is the abandoned red schoolhouse, more woods, a glimpse of the lake through the trees.

He looks over the schoolhouse from its steps to its bell tower. No one has lived there for years, though the place is well-kept—its crabapple color looks new, barely weathered, and its window-panes glow faintly white in the dusk. Once, Bill climbed the steps and peeked in the windows, half-expecting to see slates and desks filmed with dust, but instead he saw big empty rooms, a fireplace, couch marks on the carpets. In the back of the schoolhouse was even a patio deck.

Bill talks to Delia in firm, soothing tones. He whistles and takes a few steps up his drive. Behind him, a door slams. He faces the schoolhouse.

In the dim evening light, he sees a form at the window. A shadow shifts, billowing the curtains. The shadow moves past one window, vanishes, reappears in another. A light from inside carves the shadow into curves, shapes a head, arms, and ponytail. The figure bends down and rises again, holding something. In its arms are long cylinders, like rolled blueprints, or guns.

When the sun rises, before Lynn wakes, Bill laces his boots. He pockets his ancient, pearl-handled pistol—a gag-lighter-sized .25—bought after his stint in the army, when he was still wet behind the ears. Over the years, the gun has sat in his glove compartment during his long drives as a sales rep, or hung in his jacket pocket on family vacations, tucked away from Lynn's sight and the reach of his sons. Even with the safety off, the pistol wouldn't do much, its bullets harmless as b.b.s unless fired point-blank. But the gun's small weight steels his legs, stretches his back and neck into confident lines, offering just enough ballast to shift, if needed, the balance of things.

Delia sniffs his boots and begins running circles, but Bill throws her a ball. Tending the dog could slow him down, and he can't leave Lynn unprotected. He hasn't told her about the schoolhouse; these days, she worries too easily and doubts him too often. Besides, all he is doing is checking their property—walking the perimeter, as his old sergeant might say.

In the yard, he inspects the boat and the cars in the carport for invasion but nothing has been touched. He crunches through knee-high drifts to the drive. The snow this winter has been so heavy and wet that Bill could only push it into lopsided mounds. One morning after a two-foot storm, a county snowplow lumbered in, clearing his drive from the main road to the lake. Bill had been delighted—what service!—but the plowman simply laughed. "Just doing my job," he said. "You're on my grid." The plowman explained that Bill's dirt drive belongs to the county—it was a lonely and isolated, but public, road. Anyone could pull up whenever they liked, practically to their door.

Walking through the woods, he sees no signs of damage. At the mailbox, fat flakes of snow flutter down. Bill appraises the schoolhouse. Towards the back, he can see the hood of a car, something tiny and round like his wife's old Chevette. The front steps have been shoveled. The curtains are drawn.

Something crunches towards him. Around the side of the house comes a woman, small-framed, ponytailed. Her coat is thin and she wears tennis shoes.

The woman walks to the front of the schoolhouse and stops, her back to Bill, hands on her hips. Her head moves as if she's taking in every corner. He watches, unsure. Should he approach, introduce himself? The woman looks harmless, but is she alone? After all, the paper once reported a pair of lovers with shotguns—*Missouri's Bonnie and Clyde!*—who stole rings, even flowers, all the trappings for their wedding. Sure enough, a second crunching approaches.

"Mom?" A child, all hood and boots, plods to the woman and stands at her elbow. "Mom, come around back. Mom?" Mittens tug at the woman's arm. "Mom. Come on." The voice twangs pleasantly: *Moum, come awun.* Bill listens for more footsteps, but there are none.

"Hello!" he calls. The child and woman turn quickly. "I'm Bill Kelsey." He steps through a snowdrift into their wide, sloping yard.

The woman pulls the child to her hip. Her face looks young—she can't be more than a teenager—with splotchy red cheeks and caked mascara. Black shows through the blond of her ponytail. Her eyes move over Bill's jacket, down his legs, up his chest, then narrow.

"I live down the road. See, there's my mailbox," he says.

The woman squints at the name on the box. She softens and smiles. Her teeth are little, like baby-teeth.

"Well, Jesus, Bill Kelsey," she says with a laugh. "You about scared the pee out of me." Her voice is salty and reminds Bill of the truck stop waitresses who worked the outreaches of his old territory. The child laughs air clouds from its hood. Because the coat is pink and puffed, he guesses the child is a girl.

"I'm Crystal Gaines, and this is my Lucy. I guess we're neighbors. Meet Mr. Kelsey, Lucybabe. You in there, girl?" Crystal pulls on the hood and Lucy's head pops free. Her eyes are huge and denim blue. Bill calculates: his new neighbor must have become a mother at around age fourteen.

He kneels and reaches out his hand. "Pleased to meet you, Lucy."

Lucy buries her face against her mother's leg. "She's a shy one, huh, Lucybabe," Crystal laughs. "Bill, do you know anything about pipes? I think mine are froze."

He thinks of the home repair videos Lynn orders on-line. "Well, I don't know if I can offer much."

"Could you maybe just take a look? Seems a man might find something that I didn't figure."

Crystal raises her eyebrows, imploring, but her eyes sparkle. Bill wonders if she might even wink. He feels his cheeks flush. He has always maintained a polite, chatting distance with clients, coworkers—in Grand Rapids, neighbors were a wave from a patio, a shouted *Hello, there!* while mowing the lawn. Good fences, that's what Lynn always said. But this woman wears a windbreaker, no hat and no scarf. Her hands, bare and red, touch Lucy's hair.

"Well, I could take a look." He makes a show of looking at his watch. "But my wife is expecting me for breakfast soon."

Crystal smiles and takes Lucy's mitten. He follows them up the steps of the schoolhouse, through the heavy oak front door.

Inside, the floor is scattered with boxes, doll clothes, dolls, and quilts. The house smells of long-settled dust and fresh fire. Bill asks when they moved. As he talks, his breath puffs in clouds. His foot catches on the carpet, a speckled brown wool worn in spots to the padding. They walk into a room and stand at a trough-sized metal sink.

She turns a spigot to full blast. Bill watches. She leans so close he can smell her: baby powder and sweat. They both wait for a drip.

"I'm afraid this is out of my league," Bill says, finally. "Could you call a plumber?" He wonders if she has a phone—or even a phone jack—that works.

Crystal creaks the spigot off. She blows hair from her face. "Never should've let that dumb-ass hunter watch this place," she grumbles, more to herself than to him. "Told him to drip it when it's cold out, just enough to keep it moving." She sighs, a long, sliding noise that leaves her deflated. Her black-blond hair slips in her eyes.

Bill imagines her shoveling the walk, lifting the heavy snow piles with her thin, tired arms. She can't weigh more than ninety pounds. He can picture her sifting through boxes to find quilts for Lucy, hauling in wood—From where? Did she chop it herself?—building a fire alone. He thinks of the shadow last night at the window, the long dark shapes in her arms: kindling. He feels like he is walking through snow in her tennis shoes, wrapped in that shivery coat, searching for answers to a house without water as Lucy plays quietly, snow-angeling the drifts.

"You know, if you need to, you could stop by our place," he says. "Until you get this fixed."

Crystal flashes her tiny teeth. "Why Bill Kelsey, you good Samaritan. I tell you what, I might do that." She walks out of the room. Bill follows her to the front door. He steps out in the snow and crosses the road, turning once to wave Lucy goodbye.

"So now they'll be marching over to shower, run a few loads of laundry?" Lynn drops bread in the toaster. "Really, William. I don't think that was so smart." She opens the refrigerator and looks inside.

Bill gazes out the window at the frozen lake. "Sweetheart, they have no heat, no water. No one else lives near them but us." Their own first apartment had a ceiling that peeled, a huge rust-stained bathtub, wall cracks like webs. "If you'll remember, Glenn Avenue wasn't exactly a palace."

Lynn walks to the stove, cradling butter and eggs. "Well, yes. Sunny-side up?" Bill nods. "It's just we don't have any idea who she is, where she came from. I mean, what on earth is she doing way out here? By herself?" She cracks eggs and the skillet sizzles.

"Maybe she ran away, maybe her parents disowned her." He imagines Crystal strapping Lucy into a car seat, speeding off in the night. He drums the table. Delia comes wagging, drops a ball at his feet. "Can you imagine being pregnant when you were four-teen? Having that pimply kid's baby? What was his name, with the Adam's apple?"

"Henry Fike," Lynn says. "And his neck was just skinny." The toaster pops and she walks over to it. "Besides, I would never need to run away. I was a good girl."

This is something Bill can't deny. Lynn was a good girl; that's what had made her so interesting. Her hemlines fell lower, her French roll was pinned tighter, and her sweaters hung looser than any girl Bill had known. He still thrills when he remembers how she left Spikey Fike at the hayride and walked off with him—claimed Bill, so boldly, right there, before everyone. Later, she would sit at the counter while Bill jerked sodas. She would listen to him read sonnets and question the world. At the drive-in, when he wondered if God really existed, she covered her head, waiting for lightning to strike. When it didn't, she clung to him. He had been able to make her believe what he said. She believed if she waited for him to return from the army, she would be a professor's wife. Her faith embraced everything. Now, as she slides the toast to a plate, her hair catches light, and for the first time he sees gray streaks threading brown. He walks up behind her and kisses her ear.

"Going natural these days?" he whispers. Her neck smells of Ivory soap.

She laughs, tilting her head back until her lips press his. "You started this 'natural' kick. Don't forget it."

Her mouth is firm and quick and then gone, like always. She butters the toast in jerking strokes, one-two-three on each slice, and hands him the plate. She may as well be standing in their Grand Rapids kitchen, brisk and focused, impenetrable: handing out lunches, pouring cereal for the boys, steering each of them out of the door to the bus and to work. Bill returns to his chair. He once imagined that a slower-paced life—a new life—would ease her, would loosen her shoulders, smooth the pinch of her mouth. Driving the long roads of his territory, wondering how she might soften, he remembered the look on her face when she sat at his soda counter, listening. She had been enraptured. Taken. He recalled his childhood dream—a life alone in the woods—and it all came together, this place, their retirement home. Nothing around them but trees and stillness, broken only by birdcalls and his voice, reading beauty. Lynn would sit by him and sigh like she used to and they'd almost have it, the life they'd intended, before Andrew was born, and Bill took the corporate job, before Kevin was born and Bill needed a raise.

Now Lynn stands at the sink, scraping eggs from the pan. She doesn't sit by him, and she doesn't sit still. Instead, she recovers old furniture, refinishes cabinets, researches dinner recipes on the computer. She writes long letters to friends back home. She drives off to fabric stores, shaking her head at the meager selections in town—with a grandchild on the way, she says, she has a deadline, and Bill would never guess how hard it is to appliqué. As Bill reads later and later into the night, he finds himself alone when he wakes—Lynn has begun rising with the sun. Sometimes he passes her on the steps as he heads for bed, where the sheets are tucked neatly, the pillows patted and stacked.

There is a knock at the side door and Lynn's eyes meet his. "Mr. Kelsey?" a woman's voice calls. "Hey, it's Crystal Gaines. From up the road, remember?"

Crystal stands at the door, holding a basket of clothes. Lucy squats at her feet and pokes snow. Bill beckons them inside. "Sorry to bust in on you," Crystal says. Her hands fret the plastic squares of the basket. She seems keyed up. Under her eyes are black smudges.

"We had nothing to wear at all, and this body needs a change. Phewee!" Crystal holds her nose, then holds Lucy's. Delia sniffs at Lucy's boots as they walk through the door.

Lynn comes up behind them and puts her hand on Bill's back. After a silence, she introduces herself. "How are you getting along with your move?"

The narrow hallway crowds them together. Bill steers the group to the laundry room, and Crystal sets her basket on the dryer. "Well, I tell you Lynn, it's been crazy. Nothing's been right since I hauled my self down here. Best thing about it's been the car ride. Lucybabe, that doggie won't hurt you. Pet it. Bet it's soft." Lucy clings to Crystal's leg. Delia sneezes.

"Toy collie, right?" Crystal asks, kneeling. Bill nods, surprised she knows the breed. She runs Lucy's hand over Delia's fur, then lifts a paw and frowns. "Needs her nails clipped. Hell, these are long enough to paint." She coos to Delia, baby-talks. "You clicking like a tap dance doggie! Tap dance doggie, yes!" Delia wags.

Crystal stands and flips her bangs. "I could do them, if you want. I'm a groomer."

Bill cannot read Lynn's expression, the odd puckering of her eyebrows. Lucy pats the air above Delia's head.

"There you go, Sugar. Pet the doggie." Crystal looks at Bill. "That's my plan for when we get settled, set up a real nice grooming parlor. With boarding."

A grooming parlor on county road HH-10? Bill looks at Lynn, who looks like she might laugh. He tries to imagine the mongrels of Ozark County in ribboned, poodle haircuts. He smiles and waits for the rest of the joke. People are always pulling his leg.

"I'm serious as a heart attack," Crystal says. "It's a done deal. See here." She pulls a blue folded sheet from her pocket. It is a flyer: two smiling dogs hold a banner that reads, *SNIPS AND NAILS AND PUPPY DOG TAILS. Crystal Gaines, Proprietor, Professional Groomer.* In the bottom corner, a flag unfurls from a cat's tail: Purr-fect Dog Runs! Opening Soon!

"My best friend Jonelle, you'll meet her, she did the artsy stuff."

The flyer looks professional, sharp and glossy, like the pamphlets Bill used to leave with his clients. When the economy sank, he'd had to leave just a few since management was cutting corners. Looking at Lucy, whose coat sleeve is frayed, Bill wonders, Where does she find the money?

Crystal seems ready to bubble over. Reading over Lynn's shoulder, she giggles. "'Proprietor.' Been called lots of things in my time, but nothing like that!"

Lynn says, "I'd imagine."

Bill is getting uncomfortable. He finds himself staring at the flyer. "What's a dog run?" he asks.

Apparently, there are all kinds of dog runs, and Crystal describes each in detail. She tells them her brother and his friends will be arriving tomorrow to build some intricate system of tunnels and cages. "You got to have walls and a roof out here in these parts." Crystal combs Delia's fur with her fingers. "Keep the critters away and the rain off your noggin."

"Who's coming tomorrow?" Bill asks. He wants to sit down. He sees his laundry room packed with teenagers, tracking mud, drinking Pabst.

"My brother, Harlan. He's good. Knows his sawblades. And then a few other guys." Suddenly, her hand moves along Delia's ribcage. "Say Lynn. Your doggie's got her a scratch."

Lynn looks at Bill. He shrugs.

"Here," Crystal takes Lynn's hand. "Feel it? It's probably nothing to stew on. You should get her checked, though. I know a guy."

With a delicate twist, Lynn shakes off Crystal's hand. She smiles primly. "I'm sure it's nothing. I take care of my dog. Thanks for pointing it out."

"Sure thing," Crystal says. She stands up slowly and nods her head. "I know just exactly where you folks are coming from." She faces Lynn, meets her eye. Smiling broadly, Crystal says, "It's so gosh-darn nice of you to let me in with my wash! Sakes alive, I thought I'd have to find me a rock by the creek!" Her voice has become a banjo, unstrung. Was she talking like this before? She lifts something glittery from the basket and slaps it into the machine. Crystal catches Bill's eye. "Yes indeed-y. Glory be! I surely owe you one."

Then she pokes Lucy's ribs, making her laugh. "Poor little Lucy with nothing to wear. Huh, girl. You might as well be naked." Her laugh, harsh and chesty, bounces off the laundry room walls, echoes through the hallway as Bill walks towards the living room. Her voice follows him all the way to the couch, through the kitchen and den and bedroom. He lights his pipe and walks to the bookshelves, but Crystal's voice seems to find him wherever he goes.

A few days later, Bill is returning from the store when Crystal flags him down.

"Hey Bill," she calls as he rolls down his car window. "Got a favor to ask." Lucy sits in the snow. Their driveway is crowded with pickup trucks. On one bumper Bill sees what looks to be a sticker of the Confederate flag.

He works his voice into a smooth affability. "Sure thing. What can I do for you?"

Crystal stands at his window. "Here's the deal. I got to run to Daleyville to pick up some groomer stuff. Leashes, collars, assorted whatnot. Anyway, Lucy needs a nap, but they—" she looks towards her house, "are pounding the bejesus out of the back. A body can't rest in there, least of which, this body." She touches Lucy's head. Lucy's eyes are red and watery, and she pushes Crystal's hand away.

"Think she might borrow a quiet spot at your place? Just for an hour or two?"

Bill tries to imagine what Lynn will say. If she'll even speak. They've barely been talking since Crystal did her laundry. Lucy looks up at him with a weariness well beyond her years. It's the same exasperation he remembers seeing in his boys when they were worn down and mystified, when he would have to explain missed connecting flights, meetings running long: the world of adult complications.

Crystal starts tapping her hand on the roof of his car. He sighs. Maybe Lynn will feel grandmotherly towards Lucy. Maybe she won't mind at all.

He says, "I think that will be fine. You go on. No problem."

"Thank you, Lord," she says to the sky. In Bill's ear, she whispers, "Tell Lynn we won't make it a habit." With a little laugh, she straps Lucy into Bill's backseat, tells her to be good, hands Bill a blazing yellow Winnie-the-Pooh backpack, and runs to her car, waving frantically, shifting gears, pulling away.

When Lynn walks out to help him carry in groceries, she looks irked when he shushes her, raising his finger. Lucy is already asleep in the backseat. He updates Lynn in a quiet but wildly encouraging voice. He hopes that talking in whispers will somehow soften the situation.

Lynn's whisper comes out more like a hiss. "What on earth were you thinking? Honestly, William. We are not a daycare."

He silently lifts two bags of groceries from the trunk. "It's one afternoon, Lynn."

She reaches hastily into the trunk, then corrects herself. Bill can see she is torn between scolding him and worrying about Lucy, who is only a child after all, innocent, asleep. "How do you know it's only one afternoon? First it was only laundry. Next week—"

"Next week is next week. What, do you have plans?"

She looks surprised. He hasn't spoken a cross word to her since they moved.

He tries to sound apologetic. "Lynn, dear, this girl needs a hand. I'm just trying to help."

"So that's what you call it. Helping."

He takes a bag and walks ahead of her. His jaw tenses as he whispers, "Would you call it something else?"

Lynn lifts the last of the groceries and closes the trunk, slowly, in a click. She walks to the house.

She sets the bags on the back porch. He stands at the door. Neither of them is willing to leave Lucy outside alone; neither is willing to step inside. They stare at each other.

Lynn crosses her arms. "Fine then. You go on and help. Add her to your list of good intentions."

Her eyes are like Lucy's just moments ago: blunted, far away. He wonders what she must see. He was supposed make things happen and he hasn't. The long hikes together through the bramble remain paths he has to clear. The wildflower garden and vegetable patches await the till. Their quiet boat-rides up the lake instead swarm and buzz with jet skis, or else the boat engine sputters and they're left adrift in ways he cannot fix. Lynn never says so but she makes it clear, she always makes it clear, that she is going along with him, settling for less. But they were here, as promised, in the woods, no kids or work to fill them up. Things weren't really so far off, were they? Wasn't it a start?

Lucy stirs in the backseat. She is waking, confused. *Where am I?* her frown says. She starts pulling the door.

Bill goes to get her. Lynn stands at the back door, watching. "This place is full of alligators, William. Mark my words. Feed them once, look what happens. Always back for more."

He reaches into the backseat and gathers Lucy. "Well, I'm not some fat schnauzer chained up in the yard," he mutters. "I am not a snack."

He knows his words sound ridiculous and puny, that his wife has gone inside. He lifts Lucy, cradling her head, and pulls her hat around her ears. In his back, there's a creaking; he is unused to this weight. Lucy smells like his memory of all spent children, of wool and sweat-damp hair. She makes a small sound into the shoulder of his coat. As he walks up the porch steps, Delia yawns. The dog follows him inside.

Weeks pass. Bill falls behind on his reading. Every few days, Crystal comes by with her laundry and her voice blasts over the hum of the spin cycle as she talks to Lucy, to Delia, to Bill. Sometimes she brings her grooming kit and fusses over Delia. Lynn won't even stick around to be polite. In fact, his wife is always in some other room, upstairs, leaving Bill to scald soup and burn toast. To top it all off, Lynn won't let the dog come outside with him, and now Bill has to walk alone to the mailbox. Whenever he laces his boots, Lynn holds the dog on her lap and whispers sappy things. "Daddy will just get you scratched again," she says. "And we wouldn't want Crystal to scold us."

Lines have been drawn between them now, and Bill tries to smooth them. Heading out this morning for pipe tobacco, he caught sight of his wife clacking on her keyboard. It was literally the first time he'd seen her in days, and Bill missed her. Even during his years on the road, she seemed closer somehow, kneading his shoulders before he left, tucking nice notes into his suitcase. On the phone, she would fill in gaps about the boys and prepare him to return: tell him how Andrew broke his hand playing basketball, how Kevin wanted a cast so badly he'd hurled himself from a tree, and how both boys needed cheering up—maybe he could bring home football tickets? But now she doesn't arrange his vitamins by the coffeemaker with a note that says, "Take me, I'm yours." She isn't asking him to help close the sticky front window or reading him letters from their daughter-in-law. Standing there this morning, watching her type, he couldn't even catch her eye. So he cleared his throat and, in his most Shakespearian voice, asked if she would care to join him anon?

"Let's see," she answered. "Do I want to ride an hour to town to fetch some grits at the general store?" She kept her eyes on the computer screen, where Bill could see pictures of cheerful airplanes. "That's more in line with your friends up the road. Why don't you ask them."

As he gathered his keys and wallet, Delia stared at him and did not wag her tail. Under his breath, Bill said something sharp, then left. He had felt, as Crystal might put it, completely full up.

Now he drives towards the main road, towards the schoolhouse, which has been painted yellow with bright cartoon pets. It feels good to get away. He lets his mood lighten as he thinks about Lucy. She adores her new house, and out of everyone, Lucy has chosen Bill as the person she most wants to tell about it. It is the only thing he looks forward to. When Crystal comes over, Lucy draws pictures for him and tells long, clever stories: how the cartoon kitties misbehave when no one's around, how the doggies climb from the house walls and enjoy all sorts of adventures. He is thinking of her story about a parrot and a beagle, almost smiling, when he has to stop. His dirt drive is blocked. He gets out of his Range Rover and counts the trucks. Four. All pick-up trucks, loaded with wood.

He can't pull around. There isn't enough space and since the snow has melted, the mud is deep and thick. He steps gingerly through the muck and crosses the road to the schoolhouse. Since the men arrived to build the kennels, Bill has not been by. When he reaches the front door of the schoolhouse, no one answers the bell. He heads around to the patio, where he finds six men sitting around a table, poring over a sketch. None of them looks familiar. Even though it is barely ten in the morning, many of them hold beers. The men look up. They regard him with a recognition that leaves him unsettled. How much has she told them about their lives?

"Hey, Mr. Kelsey," says one man Bill has never seen. "What can we do you for?"

"Hello. Yes. I'm Bill Kelsey. And I seem to be stuck."

"Need a haul?" asks another man with blue eyes shaped like Crystal's. Some of the men wear hunter's coveralls, others heavy coats. Bill isn't sure if it is all the layers, but to a man, each one looks huge.

Crystal and Lucy appear to be gone. Bill imagines if Crystal were here, she'd whap these men upside the head. She says she has done as much before. Over laundry, she complains about how they haven't fixed her sink, warmed her pipes, relit her pilot light.

"Cousins," she'll sigh. "Dull as ladles, those boys. But good to me, when I yell."

Now Bill must explain the situation to these big, young men. He addresses them as he might his grown sons: not complaining, not forceful. The drive needs to be kept clear, he says, since it is the only way he can get out. He jokes that he and his wife are homebodies, but they nonetheless get hungry. He laughs good-naturedly and calls them "fellas." He claps together his shearling gloves.

The men stare at him for several moments. Their eyes narrow. Bill feels his smile cracking. Has he said something wrong? They look at each other, then as a body, rush towards him. Startled, Bill reaches for his jacket pocket. He steps back as the men draw near.

But he slips and falls on a patch of ice and bangs his knee. The men fly past him in a whoop. He tries to right himself, but can't get his footing. When he hears engines revving, he realizes that the men were never mounting an attack. They were racing each other to move their trucks.

The blue-eyed man has stayed behind and helps Bill to his feet. "Hey," he says. "Hey, Mr. Kelsey. Watch your step now. It's slick."

Bill stands and dusts off snow. He is embarrassed and bruised and grateful he didn't do anything foolish just now. His feet slide around on the icy deck.

"Sorry about that. Took us a full minute to understand what you were saying," the man laughs. He introduces himself as J. P. "Guess we're not used to Northern accents down this way. You all use so many words when you could make it simple."

The men return and soon everyone is apologizing. They say Crystal gives awful directions, that she's a mean boss who never feeds them enough. They joke about unionizing. They offer him a beer and seat, but Bill declines. He really has to be on his way.

Then J. P. asks about Bill's boat, which he has seen on his drives down the county road—the road that is Bill's driveway. J. P. says he's sure like to go out fishing when the weather clears, and Bill's boat looks plenty large. The other men ask why J. P. needs a big boat when all he catches is crappie, and not too many, at that. Bill's knee hurts too much to stand much longer. Things feel out of balance. The ground seems to be shifting under him, giving way. He tells the men he has to go and they say, "Later."

He limps across the road. His driveway is rutted by wheel tracks and spatter. His car windshield is sprayed with mud. He knows there's a line between carelessness and malice, favor and habit, hope and resignation. Once things crossed over, could they cross back? Bill sits in his car and rubs his knee. He thinks of Crystal sorting her clothes in their kitchen, letting Delia outside without asking. He imagines this fellow, this J. P., pulling up to Bill's door with pole and tackle. At the same time, he can see one of those men tinkering with the boat engine until it stops cutting out; he can hear Lucy asking which crayon is his favorite, then printing his name all over the page. Sitting inside his muddied car, he can even see himself breaking ground for a garden. What happens next is harder to picture. It seems strange, but he has never imagined what might be planted, the tomato vines or drooping sunflowers. He has never imagined Lynn among the rows, pulling carrots or laying fence, stuffing scarecrows. How much he wants to place her there. Already the snow is thawing. Bill squints through the mud on his windshield and tries to clean it with his handkerchief, but he only smears the view. The drive home is rough, over deep grooves and new tread, and he has to lean out the window to see his way clear.

weights and measures

How He Tells You:

When your Dad says Sit down, I have something to tell you, you imagine he'll say: I've lost my job, we're moving, you're starting eighth grade in Vermont. His voice has that something-bad's-coming sound, and he stoops to pick something off of the carpet. Of course, it's just a penny or a leaf from the fern, but he keeps looking at it while your heart squeezes still. He keeps looking at it as he tells you Your mother and I are not going to be living together anymore. I've got an apartment. That's all you hear, that and the word Separation. Not Divorce, no you listen for that as best as you can until your eyes start to cloud and make diamonds of lamplight.

You say, I'm going upstairs for a minute and your mom follows you, but her nose is all red and her undereyes puff. You don't want your mom to cry with you so you shut it off, just shut everything off and reroute the pain to your fingers. That feels better, removing the pain from your heart. She tries to hold your hand but it hurts so you pull away.

Then your Dad calls from the steps, Honey? Let's go see the apartment, and you feel your legs moving, carrying you down to his voice. The car ride is quiet. Out the windows are gray tarpatched streets, gray sky, Stop-N-Go, Marathon. Four stoplights from your house he turns the car. After two speed bumps you're parked by a door, a brown ugly steel door in a tan ugly building, flat and lonely and square as a Monopoly house. You don't know what to say, what he wants to hear. All you can see of your mom is the seat in front of you and the crumpled corners of Kleenex. Somewhere deep in your belly is an ache just like hunger, but you shut that off too, you won't feel that either. C'mon, let's look inside, your Dad says like you've rolled into Disneyworld, but instead of mermaids or dwarves you see only that door, his hand jingling keys and the colorless sky.

How to Measure Yourself:

Look. In the mirror, there's nothing but doughy goose pimples. There should be hollows punched in the sides of your hips, shadows along your shoulders and cheeks, ribs like a xylophone instead of breasts. Try pulling the flesh of your thighs, pinching the sag of your underarms to see what you'll look like in just a few pounds. Suck breath to make your pelvis a skin-covered bowl. Make your collarbones sharp as a wooden hanger. Erase borders and outlines, pull yourself tight as you'll go, turn your skin into blankets tucked into your bones.

How to Eat Sunday Dinner:

Your dad comes over for dinners on Sundays. Four stoplights away means a new zip code, a new telephone number that your mom always forgets so that you have to dial, sometimes leave a message. You feel weird calling him, asking when he'll be over, what time you should put in the pot roast, set the oven on broil. Talking to him on the phone isn't like talking to the boy from Six Flags. Your dad's voice is tinny and leaves gaps where you think it should laugh or ask questions.

When he walks through the door, your new puppy goes crazy and spins, chasing its tail for what seems like an hour. You stand at the counter sprinkling cheese on potatoes, waiting and not waiting for him to hug you. Your mom cuts tenderloin with a shrieking electric knife. You set the table wrong, knives and forks opposite, and he notices, says You never get this right, do you Honey? He pats your back and switches the silver and laughs, clinking spoons.

He brings over wine, tells of his new wine-tasting class, of the sweet whites like perfume, the reds bitter as blood. The way that you taste it, he says, is like this, and he smells the cork, pours a glug, sniffs, swirls the glass, takes a sip. You practice this with water sometimes when he leaves. He lets you have a glass with your dinner and you take little sips, your fingers wobbly on the stem of the glass, searching balance. His favorite wine tastes as pure as green apples. It has three long German names, all p's and tz's, but you recognize it at the grocery and slip splits in the cart.

At the table, he always compliments your potatoes, asks about day camp and that what's-his-name boy from Six Flags, and you talk of your puppy and arts-n-crafts classes, show him the Indian-bead pouches and frogs carved of soap. Then he asks your mom about work and they talk for awhile, and you cut your steak into slivers and move peas around. When he's finished you and your mom clear the table, pouring the last of the wine in his glass. He sits in the chair by the T.V. like he used to and clicks through baseball and news. Your mom rattles and clangs plates in the sink. You run upstairs, jam your stereo, drink a big glass of water and lock the bathroom door.

After ten minutes you return with a smile scrubbed minty white, and your dad kisses you on the forehead before saying goodbye.

How to Answer When Your Mom Asks Honey, Are You Eating Enough:

Take a bowl from the cupboard, pour in milk, swish it around so the sides are covered. Let it puddle the bottom. Sprinkle Raisin Bran in the milk, smear the bowl with stray flakes.

Coat a spoon with the milk. Leave the bowl in the sink.

Leave a glass crisped with orange juice pulp right beside it.

How to Talk to a Boy:

The what's-his-name boy from Six Flags calls while you're doing evening sit-ups, two months from the day that your dad moved away. His voice crackles and you hear girls in the background, screaming and giggling for his attention. He talks of his awesome game today, add in, add out, elbows and forearms wound tight as a spring. You sigh and laugh at his pauses and lilts, picture him in a heavy oak phone booth behind the camp commons, tan, missing you, plunking in quarter after quarter. At Six Flags he held your hand on the Gravity Smasher, his fingers callused but gentle as they stroked your own. The hair on his arms glowed like dew in the sun.

He asks What's up? but you don't tell him about day camp—it's too little-kid and he'll drive in two years. You tell him about your new puppy, how it chews table legs and chases its tail. His laughter tickles your insides, makes you giggle too, like when he asked for your phone number on the Carousel horse. Whispering I want to call you, Please I miss you already, his lips brushed your neck, and you said I don't even know you! but leaned into his arms, breathed his Polo and sweat and the warm, candied breeze and glided with him through the air until dark.

You tell him that your parents are pests, that your mom won't leave you alone. She keeps telling me to gain weight, you say, nonchalant though you secretly thrill. Then the sound of the girls in the background swells and one yells his name. He says he can't hear you so you shout, My mom is trying to make me gain weight. You hear muffling and squeals, fumbling noises. His voice returns, asking Gain weight? How much? When you tell him two pounds, he says Oh, that's all, Just eat two pounds of hamburger. You don't tell him you've lost ten pounds this month, that you weigh less now than you did in fifth grade. All you manage to say is It's not that easy—before his voice clicks off and silence buzzes your ear.

How to Gain Two Pounds:

Wear baggy shirts, loose shorts, heavy sneakers or sandals.

Heap food on your plate, cut it up, hide some in your napkin, take small bites.

Leave empty slots in cookie boxes, egg cartons. Give food to the sink or your dog or the squirrels.

If you have a scale that records your weight, hold ashtrays, hairdryers, wet towels as you stand.

If your mom follows you to the scale and watches, keep your shoes on and carry plenty of change. Under no circumstances can you let her see you naked. Feign disgust, cry pervert if she even asks.

How to Tell Your Friends:

Kate and Megan pass a cigarette on the steps after school, trying not to shiver in the newly chill air. Kate can french-inhale and makes sure everyone knows it. Megan takes the cigarette and drags and exhales, and her knees bounce into Kate's as they sit. You stand beside them playing your hands on the banister. Across the concrete, ninth-grade-boys-intramurals scuff and dodge the hoop.

Kate talks about Mr. Binder, how he always humps desk chairs when he lectures Integers, pushing stretched polyester into wood with his knee. It's so gross, she rolls her eyes. His crotch is all bulgy and he shows it to everyone. I'm like, What the hell?

Gross, echoes Megan. She blows a thin stream of smoke to the clouds. Her lipstick kisses blot the Marlboro's filter.

Kate says, And he always does it in front of Matt. I mean, God! She laughs squinty-eyed and dangles the cigarette from her lips. Her hair shimmies around her face like always, like in a movie, glinting sun, swirling over her cheekbones. Your hair itches in its plain white scrunchie.

Megan looks up at you and points at your foot, which looks boxy and big as a Tonka truck next to hers. Your boot is untied, so you stoop to lace it, but your body recalls a more functional bend. Juices pool under your tongue, in your cheeks. A familiar lurching starts in your throat. You swallow hard and stand fast, but in your mouth, sour water seeps into corners and clots. Searching the ground, you imagine your tongue as the dry, rough concrete, the sand of an anthill, the chalked lines of the court. You try making a sponge of your words, sopping puddles with talk.

Mr. Binder, the Boof-er, you offer through tightly clenched teeth. You like Mr. Binder's beard, his kind eyes, but repeat what you've heard at the back of the bus. Kate howls. Megan's eyes flick confusion but she laughs knowingly. She takes the cigarette from Kate and grins. You try to smile but a lemon squeezes your cheeks.

You swallow again and say He's such a perv, he likes to boofoo, you know? You aren't sure what this means but you've made your friends laugh. Something calming and cool washes over your tongue.

How to Shop For Your Family:

Remember: You are allowed to be here. Casually walk the aisles, poke avocados, pick one up, scrunch your nose. Survey the Prime Steak Selects, bloody juices pooling in cellophane fissures. Pace yourself. They have cameras and weirdly round corner mirrors.

Remember: You're not a kid but an upstanding consumer. Stroll accidentally into Aisle 23. Glance at the antacids, the anti-gas tablets, effervescents that bubble-coat various pains. Weigh your options—you are choosing the very best relief for your sick aunt, your sister. Your mom is Experiencing Gastro-Intestinal Distress. Picture her writhing in pain.

Remember: Your mom ate some bad Curried Chicken. Pluck a packful of laxatives from a shelf, grab diet gum. Hold both boxes low at your sides, near your sleeves. Prepare to inch your hands upward if your friends or your mom's friends suddenly wheel round the corner.

Remember: You are the customer, and so, always right. Smile at the cashier in Checkout Express. When she looks at you with a raised, knowing eyebrow, make your eyes questioning, naive, unaware. Convey tragedy with a glance—the sickness, the horrible, unexplained bug. Offer cash.

Remember: It's your business, only your business. Swing your bag as you walk. Smile at the bagboys, fill your nose with their sweet, hopeful aftershave, feel their eyes on your thinness. Whoosh through the electric doors into dark, into light, and pop a square of bitter white gum in your mouth.

How to Pinch and Slice:

Your dad calls Sunday morning and asks for your mom, and she closes the door to her bedroom to talk. Her voice rises and falls and it seems like she's angry, so you busy yourself making pie dough—cutting in butter, flouring the mat. Your dad likes apple pie so you've spent all morning peeling, measuring cinnamon, breathing everything in. When you and your mom baked together, you used to sneak bites of the crust, letting the soft clump of raw dough melt on your tongue. You loved it so much she'd even pinch out a special crust, brushing on milk, sprinkling sugar, baking it golden: sugar pie. But you're older now. You don't nibble, and you certainly won't sneak. Plus, the crust is double lattice so there's nothing to spare.

At the table, you will tell him about your project on France, which you worked on together a few Sundays ago. His wine tasting classes have taught him all about Europe and he always helps you with drawing, since you can't shade or do buildings. For your poster, he sketched the Eiffel Tower and grapevines and a bottle of wine, and you drew a bottle of mustard for Dijon. He kept joking that the poster looked really Nice, saying it Neece, like the city on the Cote d'Azur. You're going to tell him your project won second place in the big French Club contest and you got a cheese wheel, which you'll give to him. The pie is your way of saying merci and you would have done chocolate mousse, except that chocolate gives your dad hives. Your mom refused to let you try a soufflé, going on and on about things falling like Chicken Little. You will tell him about the what's-his-name boy from Six Flags, who called twice in the last week just to talk about music. You will set the silverware right and slice lemons for the water like you've seen on T.V.

Your mom walks out and says, Honey, your dad isn't coming. You ask why and she says, He has to go out of town. It isn't fair, you say. He had to go out of town two weeks ago. Why is he traveling so much all the sudden?

Your mom says she doesn't know, but you think you do. You say, He never seems to have plans until he talks to you. She says, in a syrupy voice like a teacher, Now honey, I know that it might seem that way, but the fact is your father does what he wants, when he wants, trust me on this. She says, We can still have dinner together, you and me, it'll be fun. We'll make it fancy, dress up, you can even raid my closet. That's just what you want, to wear your mother's big dorky clothes, look like her, smell like her, spend time in her company, when obviously nobody wants that at all.

How to Eat with your Family:

When your mom insists that you eat as a family, roll your eyes, sigh, slouch in your chair. Exaggerate your efforts to be cordial. Fail.

When she tries to be funny, don't laugh at her jokes.

When she piles on the cheese sauce, tell her you're vegan. Explain about dairy as you would a child or idiot.

When she reaches for salt, note the flab on her arm.

When she demands you eat three bites like you're a child, cut a bean into thirds. Swallow two.

When she threatens to ground you, shrug. You have nothing planned.

When you answer her questions, speak in monotone. Keep your words terse and even and flattened as staples, pinched as the bond that you happen to share.

How to Keep Your Mouth Shut:

The what's-his-name boy from Six Flags wants to stop by while you're babysitting, so you sneak him in when the kid falls asleep. It's been weeks since you and Megan doubled with him and his friend at the mall. Walking store to store, hand in hand, making fun of the old people and cheesy songs on the sound system, you knew his school's dance was coming up and you thought he might ask. Now there's still time and a reason to hope. You knock knuckles like NBA stars as he walks through the door. He tosses his jacket over a chair by the couch.

He says he's starting a band and your heart flutters thinking of it—his fingers sliding over frets, stroking strings, twanging songs penned for you. You ask, What kind of music will you guys play? wishing you could talk cooler, like Kate, swearing in all the right places. He lists off a bunch of groups to explain his band's sound. You don't recognize any, the names jumbled like Scrabble tiles, but you smile and nod, dreaming of all the words he could rhyme with your name. Imagining how he would lean down from the stage and pull you out of the crowd, sit you in the spotlight, gazing until his eyes closed on the high notes.

He checks out the videos of the family that lives there and says, Hey, let's watch a movie. You aren't sure if you should. He's not supposed to be here—the parents said no visitors—but the kid is a baby and can't talk yet to bust you. What's the worst that can happen? You're already grounded for acting surly, which you felt bad about later, when you overheard your mom crying in the shower. It took miles of running with headphones to burn through that sound. He asks, What do they have to eat around here? He wants popcorn, so you microwave a bag and bring out the bowl. He dims the lights and puts the bowl in his lap. You sit on the couch next to him, not quite touching, so close that your skin kind of hums.

You've never watched a movie with a boy in a band, so your mind is racing. You wonder how his arm might end up around you. What if he kisses you? You don't know how to breathe when you kiss, or if you're supposed to be breathing at all. Kate and Megan say you should wait to use tongue until the guy does it first. It's more ladylike, and boys like to lead.

He says, Have some popcorn. You take a handful, eating more than you should. He says, Have more, You're making me feel bad, and puts your hand in the bowl. Your throat tightens at the thought of stuffing your face, but you move your hand through the popcorn until you touch bottom. At the same time, he readjusts his hips. The bowl is sitting right on his zipper. Here, take some more, he says, guiding your hand back in. He helps you stir the kernels to get the ones with more butter. You crunch through oil and salt until your tongue feels eroded. Watch out for the burnt ones, he says, moving your hand through the bowl, digging deeper, again and again, until it jostles so much something has to spill.

Butter bleeds into the family's couch and you brush popcorn back in the bowl. The smell of salt stings your nose. He asks, Where's the bathroom so I can clean off my jeans? You tell him. Your hands are slick and disgusting. Hulls poke at your stomach. Already, your pants feel too tight.

When he returns, you smile and head to the bathroom. You run the faucet and wait for the noise of the movie. Soon, yellow-white clouds float in this nice family's toilet. You splash water on your face, blow your nose, rinse your mouth. No toothbrushes in here. Even the bathroom reeks of salt. You rinse and spit and spit and spit.

Everything still tastes slimy when he leans in for a kiss, your first kiss, so you press your lips tight. His mouth bounces off yours and he is surprised. He zeroes in again, softly now, lifting your chin like a movie star, playing his tongue over your lips. But you can't open up. Your teeth are coated in bile and the grit of fake butter, and you feel like you've gorged yourself when you weren't even hungry. You hold your breath until he says he has to go. When he leaves, he doesn't knock knuckles or even say Later—in fact he doesn't say anything, not even your name.

How to Stretch:

There is a kind of gum that fills your mouth with such flavor, such energy, that you can last hours on one little piece. Chewing sustains you when things can't be swallowed. Make do with a corner, a sliver, a taste.

How He Pulls Away:

Your dad drives up in a new car, a two-seater, pearly beige, sharply angled and so low to the ground that he twists to get out. He is taking you to shop for your mom's birthday present. On the way to the mall, he tells you to play with the radio, even find your crazy music, and you press buttons that beep and flash digital. He makes you watch the electronic dashboard, guns the engine so the RPM columns soar, turns the heat on and off and slides out the glossy cup-holder. As you wait for a train, he says he has a surprise and he pulls open a ledge between you. Inside is a tiny bottle of wine and two shot glasses that you recognize from your house.

Your dad laughs and pours, says, Pretty neat, huh? You think of James Bond. Are there machine guns in the headlights? you ask, remembering how he let you stay up with him to watch those old movies. But you also remember that in your seat would be a woman with long spidery lashes, poofy-haired and adoring. As your dad sips and watches the train chug along, you can't decide whether you like the wine cabinet or car, whether you should tell your mom about any of this. The wine is syrupy and tastes like rose petals. You and your dad count train cars like when you were little and cheer at the caboose.

At the mall, your dad says, Let's stop in here and you walk into a gleaming white jewelry store. You aren't sure why he's chosen jewelry for your mom's present after six months of Separation and Sunday dinners, and you wonder if he might want to move back, but you can't let yourself think about that so you stop. Something tinges your wrists. You clench your hands like you do when your stomach complains.

Your dad helps pick out silver earrings and says to go get some ice cream while he pays, A snack to fatten you up, Miss Skinny. On the way out, you notice your dad pointing at another counter, the salesman lifting the glass, removing a slender gold chain. You walk to the ice cream stand and order two cones of fudge-coffee, one double scooped just for him. One big, chunky bite melts in your mouth before you dump most of your cone in the trash, breaking off half the sides and crunching the rest to a crown. You hurry back to the store before his cone starts to drip.

Looks good! he says, smiling broadly, and exchanges the bag under his arm for the ice cream. Peeking inside, you see only one small gift-wrapped box, just big enough to hold your mom's silver earrings. He winks at you, licking chocolate as you walk through the parking lot, and points at your cone, saying You must have been hungry, I don't know where you put it. You break little pieces and scatter them as you walk, nibbling only when he looks over at you.

Driving home, he asks you about the what's-his-name boy from Six Flags but you have nothing new, in fact even told him last Sunday that the boy has stopped calling. He asks How's the wide world of eighth grade? and starts the same story he tells every week, about his own junior high and being picked on by seniors, about scrubbing the school seal with a toothbrush because the big kids made him, about humiliation and learning experiences. You laugh like you've never heard it. Then he says: Be nice to your mom, This is all hard on her. You think of the mysterious gold chain catching light, your mom's silver earrings nestled in a box in your lap. Maybe the chain isn't for her at all. Your fingernails bite your palms as your hands chew themselves. Turning into your driveway, he says: You have to be kind, Honey, Your mom needs you now. She has no one else.

Don't say anything. When he kisses your forehead and says he'll take you all out this Sunday for a birthday celebration, try not to ask if he'll be there for sure. Do not ask your dad for his certain return. Just reach for the door handle. Ignore the pain in your fingertips as you lift the lock. When your knuckles throb down to the tender half-moons of your nails, keep moving, open then slam the door shut. Smile as he beeps his chirpy new horn and watch him pull away. Raise your hand, wave goodbye, notice how the ache is subsiding, that it's thinning to nothing, like your breath, like air.

let's do

Estelle hadn't meant to sleep with the interviewer, but here she was, underneath him, watching his furry back heave and shudder. It was 3:30 on a Tuesday. The afternoon light leaked through the dank hotel drapes. She hadn't really looked at the room until now, as the interviewer labored and she urged him along, cheerleading him to the finish line, slapping his ass now and then. Whatever would help. The room smelled like smoke and beneath its slick bedside table, Estelle spotted a Frito, something missed by the maids. A strange constellation of stains marked the ceiling. She hated hotels, hated knowing of other sad couplings on this bedspread, the women paid or plied or taken by force, the men poking urgently at anything warm. She tried to remember the last hotel she'd been in: it was years ago, an old roadside motel on a cross-country trip with her husband, Paul, who was now moving out. It must have been Wyoming. The sky had hung low with angry black clouds and they were lost and exhausted, and when they saw the neon-lit "vacancy" sign, they both sighed. They had been young and in-love enough to laugh at the cobwebs, the fusty pictures of flowers outlined in yarn. They had slept under a quilt sewn from old dresses, curling into each other like puppies, or socks.

She had all but forgotten about that trip. A little sound escaped her throat.

"Good?" breathed the interviewer. His tongue probed her ear.

"So good," Estelle said, raking her nails up his back. She glanced at her watch, though there was no reason to, nowhere that she had to be. By now, her husband was probably home from work, packing boxes, waiting for her to return so he could claim this lamp, that chair. Or he might be unpacking at his new apartment, the first floor of a Queen Anne in the crumbling heart of the city. She hadn't seen it but he had described it in detail, the paint peeling like eggshells, the shutters askew. A fixer-upper, the kind of place she'd embraced when they first started out. Back then, Estelle had been the kind of girl who looked forward to things. There had been a voice in her head, the voice of countless Girl Fridays, primed for adventure, greeting opportunity with a melody: *Oh, let's do!* Let's do a picnic, a midnight swim, cow-tipping, marriage! Let's do our own wallpapering, drive our way out West! Then, there had been no reason to decline. Any wrong turn could be a lark, every misstep alighted in madcap charm. Let's do our kitchen in purple, buy a used German car! Error was burnished by college tries. Time had been blank and simple as a clock face, open, forgiving, its hands returning and returning her to beginnings.

Now everything laid bare the machinery of habit and regret. New shoes led to bounced checks, new neighbors to hedge squabbles. Even her favorite police drama contrived freshness by turning all its characters into vampires. Why even try? There was no mystery in the bedsprings creaking beneath her. No surprise in the interviewer's final, triumphant thrust. The only surprise, really, was that she was here. Estelle was too old and too smart to do this—pushing forty, several years out of law school. Until today, she had almost forgotten about the lower regions of her body; everything below the waist seemed like a chaotic country she had long escaped and tried never to recall. And she had no interest at all in the interviewer, with his bird legs and his money clip and his way of summoning waiters by snapping.

He rolled off of her, pulling the sheet over his penis, now life-less, a wrinkled balloon. Her breasts were carpeted in fallen chest hair.

She made herself watch as he reassembled. He bent over for socks. He wiggled into his briefs, snapped the waistband. He placed one thin knobby leg in a pant leg, hopped, placed the other. All the while, Estelle felt nothing. But on the horizon, approaching, there was a shadow: a mood was amassing like a rank of soldiers. An old and urgent sorrow would overtake her any minute. She fixed on the interviewer as he buttoned his cuffs and, aware of her eyes, nimbly tied his tie. In the mirror, he checked his teeth. Estelle's skin was goose-pimpling from the air conditioner, but she did not cover herself.

"It was nice, um, meeting you," he said, standing at the door. He clearly had no idea how to exit. She guessed she was the first job candidate he had slept with, though, she also guessed, not for lack of trying. Where would he go now? Back to the office? Home? To someone who was waiting?

"Same here," she replied. She felt a rumbling in her chest. The dark mood was advancing, tunneling in. She would have to scoot him along.

"Well then," he smiled.

They would never see each other again. She could make this easy.

"So I guess I start Monday?" she joked. His face registered alarm, then relief. He laughed and opened the door and Estelle waved him through it, smiling placidly until he was gone. She lay still and waited to be overwhelmed. In the meantime, she made herself as light and empty and useless as a riddle. If a failed lawyer weeps in the middle of a sleazy hotel room, does she make a sound?

The interview had been with a large, prestigious law firm and was arranged by Mimi, who most people knew as the Honorable Mary Williams. Estelle was Mimi's law clerk. While the Honorable Mary Williams sat unruffled as she garnished wages and denied bail, Mimi doted on her clerks, especially Estelle. Estelle had a history of attracting mothers. She had the small smile and frail shoulders of someone easily tucked under wing.

"You need to eat more," Mimi said, handing her something that looked like a brownie. Mimi baked with abandon, and lately, with a good deal of pumpkin. The brownie was orange with a candy-corn face. Estelle bit its nose.

They were on lunch break, a week before Estelle slept with the interviewer. Mimi kept offering her pita wedges and soup. It had been a wearying morning in the courtroom. Mondays were teeming with weekend rabble—wife beaters, disorderlies, petty thieves, vandals. At arraignment, belligerence and wheedling were the norm, a comfortable rhythm, almost a game: the defendants stood glaring or launched wild excuses, as the lawyers curried favor and wore far too much gel. That morning, however, the defendants had been thinner, more threadbare than usual, drooping with shame or confusion as they were arraigned. A few had families watching. Looking out at the courtroom, at the coatless babies and the solemn, dignified grandmothers, Estelle wished for one juicy assault and battery to lighten the docket. Something with teeth. But hour after hour, it was self-loathing drunks, shuffling up to the bench without counsel, repentant and wasting, a wretched parade. They were helpless and knew it. The court was just a stop on a protracted derailment. Even Judge Mary softened as she outlined their rights. "Do you have any questions for the Court?" she asked, again and again. Heads hung silently, awaiting the blade. "Are you sure? Go ahead, ask anything. We have the time."

Clerking was taking its toll on Estelle, and in chambers, Mimi said so. "You've had some hard times, kiddo," she said, meaning the babies. Estelle had lost four babies in the past few years, three during pregnancy, one just after. It was an ordeal she refused to talk about. And why should she? The last time, she had carried nearly full-term, fielding questions about due dates, describing the nursery, laughing it up at showers with pregnant neighbors, whose fat perfect babies now toddled their lawns. Everyone knew what didn't happen. A round belly and no baby: it was a blank people could fill in for themselves.

Which was why Mimi fretted over her, and why she held a clerkship usually staffed by law students, not graduates like Estelle, who'd been out for some time. Like the sad sacks who shlubbed their way through the courtroom, Estelle had been derailed. Mimi kept nudging her back on track.

"So with the stress of . . . your life, and the stress of this job, I wonder if you're feeling a little burned out," Mimi asked.

Estelle considered this. She thought about the eviction hearing last week—a mother on dialysis, a dead mailman father, between them too many crying children—and the landlord, a scumbag with the law on his side. She thought about the bald apathy of rapists, the loony loyalty of stalkers. "Maybe," she said.

"Maybe, my tooshie. Have you seen your eyes lately? You're barely in there, Estelle. You're vanishing."

Mimi touched Estelle's hand. Her skin was cool as a pillow. Estelle felt tired and struggled to stay bitter and suspicious. "You sound like you're selling something," she said.

Mimi said, "Always so cynical. But in this instance, you're right. I want you to interview at Wright, Waters, Fieldhouse next week."

This was the last thing Estelle could have wished for. In Judge Mary's court, she could engage the law from its margins, with little effort. She didn't have to be deeply involved. She spent her days recording proceedings, researching precedent, fueling juries with pretzels and sodas. She had become a gear-greaser and preferred things that way. The problem was that Mimi had known her for too long, and remembered the old Estelle, the trailblazer, the comet, who had worked here before as a fresh law student. Estelle had been expansive then, impossible to fill. But after the babies, she'd grown smaller; life seemed to be a dwindling, a closing of doors. It seemed to her that when you were young, you trotted around, sniffing everything, until life thwacked you on the nose with a rolled-up newspaper. You had to say no first.

"No," Estelle said.

"Yes," pronounced Mimi, in the voice of Judge Mary. "I've already talked with Phillip Fieldhouse, and he's expecting you. I've given you next Tuesday off. Consider it tough love."

Later that evening, as her husband filled boxes and bumped into things and cursed in the next room, she called Mimi. Mimi's son answered the phone.

"She's gone," he said, chewing what sounded like a gigantic wad of gum.

"Can you leave her a message?" Estelle asked. She could hear him fumbling around, or pretending to, for a pen.

"Go for it," he said.

"Can you say Estelle called? Then just write the word 'no' ten or fifteen times on the page."

"That's your message?" he asked. Young people had always found her weird.

"I'd really appreciate it."

"Yeah, sure, whatever."

Estelle had drifted off in her chair when the phone rang. The television was still on, and Paul had covered her with blanket. He would be decent until the bitter end. On the answering machine, she heard Mimi's voice, speaking low: "In Re your message. Yes. Yes. Yes. Yes. Yes. Yes. Yes. No more appeals."

Oh, how she hated lawyer jokes.

Driving now, red-eyed, wet-haired, reeking of hotel soap from a long, inadequate scrubbing, Estelle passed the law firm where she would never work. The building blazed in the setting sun. It seemed impossible that she had been inside there this morning, shaking hands, chatting with partners who lined up to meet her. How could it be receding now in her rearview mirror? Certainly, the day had started well. Paul had made her scrambled eggs before leaving for the high school where he taught. He continued to do small things like that, cleaning gutters, heating soup, waiting until he was really gone to move the living room couch where he slept. Estelle knew it wasn't malice that had split them—nothing with that kind of juice. Having, then not having, all the babies had gradually wrung them dry. After the last one, they had mourned silently and apart, branching off into arid loneliness like tributaries in drought.

This morning, however, Estelle felt a trickle of curiosity. Something was sliding beneath the hard indifference she'd cultivated. She drove unsnarled through morning traffic and found a good spot in the garage. She wore a sleek pinstriped suit from the back of her closet and a pretty yellow blouse. In the ladies' room in the firm's lobby, she was stunned by her reflection: an attractive, tailored professional with neatly tied-back hair. Usually, she felt neutered and dull when such women entered Judge Mary's courtroom. But yesterday after court, she decided to buy a lipstick. She blotted on a tissue. As she walked to the elevators, someone asked her for directions. A bubbling anxiety verging on thrill made her almost swing her briefcase.

The law offices were crisp and lovely, with oak-paneled conference rooms and dark studded chairs and panoramic views of the river. The elevator spoke in soothing electronic tones. She was greeted by Phillip Fieldhouse, a tall, silver-haired man who'd been Mimi's co-editor on Law Review. He escorted her through the halls and was so gallant that Estelle nearly took his arm. They walked past doorway after doorway of smiling, handsome people, wearing fashionable suspenders or tweedy skirts, arranged in various lawyerly poses—reading with glasses perched low on their noses, requesting files from the paralegals. It was a scene out of the movie Estelle used to play in her head, the scene that had propelled her through the most narcotic classes and onward through the Bar. The offices buzzed with direction, purpose, service, strategy. In the hall, the sun poured in through the giant windows, dazzling her. She imagined laughing collegially at the microwave, thumbing leather-bound torts in the library. She stood aglow with an ancient kind of hope.

Phillip deposited her at a conference room for several rounds of interviews. Her credentials impressed the first few pairs of associates. As she waited for the next group, Estelle felt relaxed, even winning.

Then, a woman she recognized from law school walked in with another silver-haired senior partner. The woman's name was Penny Franklin and during trial practice, Estelle remembered, Penny had the annoying habit of beginning every sentence with

"Okay." Penny had sounded like an airhead but booked every exam and could lacerate a mock-witness on cross-examination. "Okay, Mr. Newberry," Penny had asked Estelle's defendant during one mock trial. "Okay, so why does your statement to the police contradict your sworn testimony?"

Mr. Newberry, played by an aspiring lawyer named Hal who shared Estelle's study carrel, had mutely beaded with sweat. He was terrible at improvisation and Estelle had prepped him poorly. She had been three months pregnant at the time and was throwing up every hour, and her fictional client was a homeless ex-con who'd been caught dead-to-rights for armed robbery. Estelle had launched a Twinkie defense: Mr. Newberry's diet of sugary scraps from the dumpster had diminished his capacities. It was a stupid ploy that Penny dismantled with savage flourish. Estelle had been rankled. Now Penny was sitting across the table, trying to place her.

"Okay, I thought I recognized your name," Penny said. "Weren't we in Property Law together?"

Estelle shook Penny's hand and lied, "It's good to see you again."

"You, too. Wow, wasn't that a long time ago. How have you been?" Penny asked. She was tan and earnest and wore several jeweled rings on her manicured fingers. She made a note on Estelle's resumé with an expensive tortoise-shelled pen. Within years, perhaps months, Penny's name would be engraved on the letterhead. Estelle felt her lipstick starting to clump.

"Okay, right. Now I remember—you were having a baby," Penny said. "He must be what, about four by now?"

A perfectly normal question, but one Estelle couldn't answer. In Penny's world, in everyone's world, child-bearing ended in an actual child. Mothers-to-be became mothers. Wombs and fluids and fallopian tubes hummed along in harmony; ultrasound photos and tiny footprints were pasted in baby books. Penny probably had a whole litter by now. The senior partner next to her probably had oodles of grandchildren. The desks of everyone in this firm were probably bursting with pictures of chubby infants. Estelle thought of the nursery rhyme that had haunted her since her last baby, a sweet-faced boy who faded hours after birth: a giant shoe full of babies, poking through eyelets, swinging from laces, swallowing the tongue. The air around her grew close and hot. She wasn't supposed to be thinking like this. Not here, not today.

She clenched her teeth and said, "Actually, that didn't work out."

Penny cocked her head while the senior partner shuffled papers. Estelle could almost see her brain clicking. "Okay, well," Penny said. "I'm sorry to hear that."

"Thank you," Estelle said. "But it's all right. I mean, how could you have known?"

The senior partner smiled sympathetically. But Penny's brow furrowed like it used to in class whenever a professor refined her answers. She couldn't stand to be corrected. She became dogged and chatty and unfunny, though she often went for laughs.

"Well, at least you got your figure back," Penny said.

Estelle tried to be gracious. "Gosh. I never thought of it that way."

"My last one left me with such a belly!" Penny patted an invisible roll of fat and made a frowny face.

"How awful for you," Estelle said weakly.

"Oh, I manage," Penny laughed. "Running after a fifteen-month-old keeps me pretty fit." Then, with the false empathy and optimism of a thousand talk shows, she said, "You know, you can always try again."

The senior partner made a sound in his throat. It was clear they had crossed a line. Interviewers weren't supposed to ask you about your children. It was against the law and they knew it; these were lawyers, for heaven's sake. Whenever the issue was raised in everyday settings, Estelle demurred, asking people about their kids, letting them yammer about teething and starring roles in school plays. But sitting there, pinned and prodded by lucky, abundant Penny, Estelle shrunk into the mean kernel she'd become. She wanted to discomfit, to inflict. So she replied with the worst possible thing: the truth.

"We did try," Estelle said.

"Okay, well, I didn't realize."

"Over and over and over again."

"Gosh, I'm sorry—"

"But all of my babies died."

Penny couldn't even muster an okay.

"Every single one. Isn't that amazing?" Estelle patted her portfolio. "I think it speaks to my consistency."

Penny blinked. The senior partner scribbled on a notepad. Estelle went numb. There was no viable passage back to safe conversation, although for the next twenty minutes, conversation was performed. Penny and the senior partner asked what made her unique, and Estelle responded tersely and without conviction, like poor Hal on the witness stand. Then, she set her jaw. For the rest of the morning, as people extended handshakes and greetings, Estelle stared at the polished grain of the table. Their questions didn't matter. Nothing mattered anymore. A door had opened to a wonderful future, but she had trotted out her past—served up her anguish—just to win a point. She had guarded her memories as she would have children, keeping them close, shielding them from strangers. Now, she was the opposite of motherly. She was grotesque.

If she couldn't be trusted to protect her grief, she resolved to ride out its worst impulses. Dejection would make her powerful, self-ruinous, sloppy, loose. As Phillip handed her off to lunch with the last interviewer, an ugly man with a ready wink, something familiar in the back of her mind—perhaps it was discretion—

shook its head and turned away. Over lunch, she would drink and let the interviewer get fresh. She would feign interest in patent law. She would part her legs when the interviewer's hand fell on her thigh. She didn't deserve a future. She would screw herself out of the chance.

When Penny Franklin had asked what made her unique, what Estelle wanted to say was this: "I have a talent for wrecking things." In fact, she was endowed with a whole arsenal of destruction. There was her selfish, mutinous body. The spite that seized her whenever Paul talked about his feelings. Hostility for anyone who offered help or home-cooking. A knack for betraying the memory of lost children. Add to this an afternoon spent grinding away people's faith in her. She was like those supernatural kids who impaled priests on gateposts or started fires with their minds. Havoc. That's what she was good at. It was her specialty.

When had her world become so otherworldly? When did she set up camp there? Was it after the first miscarriage, the second? Had everything that made her normal simply bled away?

Her eyes stung and the sky was dark and she had no idea where she was going. She pulled into a rest stop so she could get it together. She blew her nose and settled into the slams and beeps and shouts of human transience. Cars pulled in and out. Dogs yanked people towards the trees. Children and grandmas unfolded themselves from backseats and ambled to vending machines. She wondered where they were all headed. Away. Home. No place seemed comfortable. Little kids ran around and stomped on one another's shadows. Moms wiped their babies' faces hard and handed them off to dads.

Maybe it was the surprise, the series of surprises, that made each next one worse. At first, when Estelle and Paul worked on the nursery, it seemed like different coat of paint was all you needed for better luck. They would lie in bed and talk about where, as kids, they had thought babies came from. Paul told her about a dream when he was four years old and his mom was pregnant. He understood babies involved love and an egg, so he dreamt that his dad kissed his mom, and when she opened her mouth, there it was, on her tongue, like a pink jellybean. The egg. His dad had given it to his mom through kissing, and she would swallow it and sprout his sister. Estelle loved the simplicity of that dream, the way two people opened their mouths and passed something sweet that grew and grew.

Of course, it was more complicated. After the second try, they decided to give themselves time. People told them about their miscarriages—school friends, professors, in-laws, even Mimi—everyone had lost, but in the end, it worked out fine. Nature was being selective, they said. You could always help by preparing a better nest. So Estelle ate three meals a day and took the year off from law school. Her husband did the heavy lifting. They took long, aerobic walks and spooned on the couch and let the past fade like a stain. They started to touch with heat.

But ten weeks into their third baby, the bleeding started again. The doctors diagnosed an ectopic pregnancy and there it was, on the ultrasound—a lump in the throat of her fallopian tube, a snake swallowing a mouse. They stopped calling it a baby so that it could be terminated. Even then, Paul held her hand through the cramping and shushed her when she blamed herself for drinking coffee, for worrying too much, for having faulty parts. They decided to adopt, and for awhile this was enough. It was a different kind of start that filled them with new energy. People told them about their adoptions. It took some time and patience, they said, but in the end it was worth it. You could always help by having lots of cash on hand. So she went back to law school and plumped her resumé with the clerkship, and Paul coached junior varsity tennis. They barely saw each other. Still, something sparked when he slid his fingers between her buttons. When she got pregnant a fourth time, they put adoption on hold. Estelle graduated. They knew their joy could topple at any minute, so they moved on tiptoes. They waited to choose a name, to decorate the nursery, to tell their parents and friends, to shop for onesies and little hats with ears, until every ghostly milestone had passed and it seemed like things had taken hold.

Estelle couldn't help crying now when she thought about it. She knew she was parked under the rest stop's floodlights, that her windows had yet to fog over. She knew she was on display for travelers like some thrashing species at the aquarium. But it was beyond her control. Late in the sixth month, the doctor said there were problems in the amniotic fluid. Which meant it was likely their son would be born with everything but lungs. Lungs? they asked, in disbelief. Who knew such things were optional? They couldn't comprehend. Her husband argued with the doctor—if their baby was incomplete, it was the doctor's job to fix it. A thing like that could be fixed, right? It was like buying a toy and realizing that the batteries weren't included. You went out and bought batteries and stuck them in and the toy burbled to life. Wasn't it just like that?

They had options, the doctor said, but surgery was not one of them. The odds for delivering a healthy baby were very, very slim. Estelle and Paul went home. They were tired. She asked her body why it hated them, why it hated all their babies. Paul said he would support any decision she made. She knew the sickness of termination. She tried to imagine what might happen if the baby was born and died. But what she saw most clearly was what would happen if he were pink and perfect. Did she want to take the chance? What a mockery of choice. With a final, weary burst of faith, Estelle had said, Oh, let's do.

Fool. She was shaking in her car and her face was a mess of wet. Stupid, stupid, stupid. What was hope but arrogance dressed up in puppy eyes? In the final weeks before delivery, their slim chance seemed to grow to a good chance because it was the only chance they had. She labored and pushed and held Paul's hand, surrounded by her parents, his parents—and their son came out squalling, a thin, high sound. Everyone laughed and cheered, saying, Wind, he's got some wind! And finally Estelle could exhale. She had made a little life. They would name him and take him home and begin for real this time; years of failure would fall away with the weight of pregnancy. Then they saw the x-ray. Instead of lungs, his trachea branched into tiny buds, a tree awaiting leaf. He would live for a little over two hours. He had ten perfect fingers and curling toes and wispy blackish hair. They named him Matthew Thomas. Holding him, she wondered what he sensed or thought, if anything. What breathing felt like without air. If he was warm or hurt or frightened. If he understood her skin.

A knock at the window startled her. A woman in a hat was motioning for Estelle to roll down her window. Wiping her eyes, Estelle could see the woman was a state trooper. She'd never seen a woman state trooper before. A twinge of pride mixed with the dread that she'd broken something else.

"Ma'am, are you okay?" asked the trooper. The trooper had freckles and a red ponytail. She had leathery skin and a boxy, authorial chest that made it impossible to tell if she was old or young.

Estelle knew she had to respond or she'd be asked to step out and walk a line. "I'm fine. I'm just trying . . . to collect myself."

"Bad day?" asked the trooper. She shined a flashlight over the back seat.

"Bad day," Estelle agreed. The flashlight blinded her, then clicked off. She was sure her eyes were the burning red of emergency flares.

The trooper asked to see her license and registration, checked them over, then handed them back.

"Can you tell me where you're headed, Estelle?"

The trooper didn't seem suspicious, just concerned in a civic way. Estelle didn't know what to say. She didn't know where she was headed.

"I guess I'm on my way home," she said, but it sounded fake to both of them. The trooper touched the brim of her hat. She looked hard through the window.

"You sure, ma'am? Is that a good idea?"

She wasn't sure. What on earth would she tell Paul? She imagined him on the couch, waiting for her to come home, as he had after the Bar exam, saying, "So? Leave anybody standing?" He had always been in her corner. He wanted good things for her. And just hours ago, she'd spread her legs for some hideous, grunting man. She felt like nothing but an ashy end, like a cigarette burned too long. She wished a good strong wind would come along and scatter her.

The trooper leaned in. "In my line of work, I see a woman like you, all worked up and alone and sitting in a car, I have to wonder if home is where she came from."

Estelle understood. The trooper was used to women in flight who kept their busted-up mouths shut. In Judge Mary's courtroom, Estelle had seen the men that hit them—wormy types who looked like they'd been kicked around a lot on playgrounds. "Oh, no. I'm not upset about that. I mean, I'm not abused." She straightened up as she remembered she was an officer of the court.

"You have someone you might call then?" the trooper asked.

She thought for a minute. It was only six o'clock but she was exhausted and couldn't imagine talking to anyone. "Maybe I could call my boss. She's a judge. Judge Mary Williams. I'm a clerk down at the courthouse."

At this, the trooper brightened. "No kidding," she said. "Do you know Rusty Weaver? In Magistrate Carlossi's courtroom?"

Estelle didn't. Lots of troopers worked the courthouse, helming security, watching the doors. The trooper seemed to know them all, was even related to a few. She talked for a good ten minutes, and Estelle was lulled by her voice, and the voices that crackled over her radio in sporadic little bursts. So much so she almost didn't hear the trooper say, "Well, Estelle, you look kind of tired. I'm off in a few. What do you say we grab a coffee?"

All she wanted was to sleep. She thought of sleeping in her cruddy backseat, as lunatic hitchhikers or the next shift of troopers knocked on her window all night. Could you really say no to a trooper? The officer, whose name was Amy Weaver, seemed friendly enough. Estelle could sit and let her talk. She could soothe her eyes before making her way to somewhere. Amy Weaver told Estelle to meet her at the pancake house at the next exit, and Estelle drove on. She sat in a booth surrounded by pictures of heaping, buttery breakfasts. She waited to feel hungry.

She'd had to mace some perpetrators in her time and had some run-ins with big men, but what really got to Officer Weaver was the expression "lady trooper." She signaled the waitress for more coffee. "It's the same thing with sports teams," she said. "What does a 'lady wildcat' look like? They put lipstick on the mascot?"

They had been sitting in the restaurant for over an hour, and as she talked, Estelle sensed she was not the first troubled motorist that Officer Weaver had met for pancakes. She could tell by the way the trooper paused and pitched to engage her audience. How her anecdotes embedded lessons. How she avoided the topics that surely sent hundreds of women driving and sobbing into the night: husbands, children, other types of defeat.

"And these women on T.V.," Officer Weaver continued. "Police detectives in lacy tank tops. Or else they're all tough and butch. You're either sexy or you're a man." The waitress refilled their cups and Officer Weaver stirred in sugar. "And don't even get me started on that show with all the vampires."

Estelle nodded. That show had gotten stupid. Could it really be so long ago that she and Paul snuggled on the couch and watched it, trying to predict which cop was crooked, which one would turn out gay? But this season, the characters had changed. They lurked in shadows and waited for prey, while Paul graded in another room or drove his boxes across town. When she found herself watching now, alone, she imagined him making fun; she could hear him saying "Oh, please!" and "Nice fangs!" like her own private laugh track. What would she do when her mind was quiet? When she sat in her chair by a blank space the size of their couch, staring at the cats?

Her parents wanted her to move back home. They were alarmed at the way her life was unraveling and suspicious of her composure. On the phone, she tried to sound forward-thinking, but they didn't seem convinced. They called her every other day.

"I'm going to sell the house," she would tell them, though she had no intention of doing so.

"Oh sweetie," her mom would reply. "Are you sure you want to be by yourself right now?"

"I'm fine, Mom. I'll get a cute loft downtown."

Then her dad would call her bluff. "Good! Tell me about the places you've looked at."

And she would act huffy, as if they were selling her short, as if they were overprotective, which they tried hard not to be. When they answered, "It's just that selling a house can be difficult," which really meant, "We worry you'll fail again," she had ways to use their doubts against them. "Great," she would say, theatrically indignant. "Now my own parents have no faith in me."

Which worked every time. Her parents would have to spend the next few minutes building her up, and once Estelle feigned confidence, the call could end on a positive note. Her parents believed in the lessons of adversity. As a family, they had weathered some tough times—a house fire when Estelle was nine, the loss of her dad's corporate job, her mom's diabetes. Throughout it all, Estelle knew, she kept them invested in life. Once, her mom had said as much. "When the house burned down and we lost everything, it was terrible. Then your grandma died, and your dad—well, we never would have made it without you, Estelle." It confirmed what she had suspected of most people: children were often the only thing that kept you from killing yourself. Your mere presence mattered. Even if you were a total bastard, they resented your absence from their lives. They worried when you went missing, got mad when you didn't show up. They gave you a reason to stay steady in a storm. She recognized that this must be the fear threading her parents' voices. That she could be as selfish as she wanted now. That she had used up her reasons for living.

"Estelle?" Officer Weaver asked. "Hello in there?"

"I'm sorry. What were you saying?"

"I was putting you to sleep with my rant about T.V. Hey, I can't eat a whole slice of cheesecake. Why don't we split one?" Before Estelle could refuse, the waitress had cleared their dishes—Estelle's picked-over pancakes, the trooper's clean plate—and taken their order.

"So how do you like working for Judge Mary Williams?" Officer Weaver asked. Her eyes were the color of overcast skies and looking at them, Estelle felt exposed. She played with the handle of her coffee cup, which, she noticed, was crusted with yolk from other people's breakfasts.

"It's fine," Estelle said. If she ever wanted to leave this restaurant, she would have to pay attention.

The trooper nodded.

"I mean, it's a little rough, sometimes. There are a lot of hard luck stories in there. And all you can really do is punish people, or start them on that road."

"That's grim," Officer Weaver agreed. "That's why I like being on the other side of the system. Being a trooper is sort of like being a doctor, I think. You see someone in trouble, you assess the danger, you get to choose a treatment. One time, I had a call to check on a disturbance at a gas station. I pulled in and saw it through the wall—you know how they have those glass walls along the front?—white male, early thirties, six-foot-five, two hundred pounds, obviously causing trouble. Some girls on a road trip were huddled by the cash register, and this guy was right next to them, screaming at the cashier, getting in his face. The cashier was a skinny kid who looked to be about ten. The tall man seemed to be waving a weapon, a piece of metal, shiny and long. So, I got ready to move in. Of course, you never know how a person is going to react, if an officer will agitate him further or shut him down or what. And this guy seemed somehow off."

The waitress sat a plate between them—a wedge of cheesecake heaped with bright canned cherries. Officer Weaver took a bite.

Estelle realized this was her cue. "Off?" she echoed.

"Yeah, different somehow. Off."

"How was he off?"

"Well, for one, he was waving his arms in a wild circle, which you get with lots of drunks and paranoids, but it was like he had no idea what was around him. Bags were knocked on the floor. The newspaper stand was tipped. It wasn't careless, but it wasn't really malicious, either. Plus, the guy never looked at me, from the minute I pulled in, and here I am, an officer in uniform, walking to the door, in plain view. Those little girls saw me right away and were pleading with their eyes. 'Get me out of here'—I've seen that look a hundred times. And the man looked unkempt but not dirty—not stained, not stubbly. That's what tipped me off. I was thinking, 'It's like he's never seen a mirror.'"

Estelle chewed a bite of cheesecake, which tasted like milky gum. Even her jaw felt tired. She worked to stay alert. Something stage-whispered in her ear: *Your next line is, "So what was wrong with him?"*

"Blind," Officer Weaver replied. "It turned out the guy was blind and extremely pissed off, pardon my French. He was waving his cane around. So I walked in like any other customer and listened to what he was saying. He didn't care. He was yelling that the cashier had shortchanged him, and demanding his money back. And guess what?"

"What?"

"He was right. One of the college girls had seen the whole incident and made a statement. The cashier had given him a dollar change out of a twenty, for a pack of cigarettes." Officer Weaver shook her head. "The blind man was a guidance counselor. He wasn't crazy. But would he have believed I was a police officer if I'd gone charging in and startled him? And if my adrenaline was pumping, would I have believed he was the victim?"

Estelle said it was worth considering. She seemed to be drifting into her own kind of darkness. She thought about what it must be like, having to listen for lies, knowing you've been wronged, when you couldn't even be sure that what you held was just a dollar bill. Growing angrier the more you knocked things over, when you were trying to set them right.

"It's all in how you look at it," Officer Weaver said, with a tinge of bromide. "A situation can be totally different once you change the view."

Estelle's interview clothes, her nice suit and heels, suddenly felt overworn. Her blouse held the stink of failure and her feet felt bruised. She needed to move on. She thought about living blind among the sighted, of crashing every single day into walls and curbs and aisles, a world arranged by unfathomable logic.

Get me out of here, she thought.

She left before Officer Weaver could order more coffee, saying she had children awaiting their bedtime stories, but that she was beginning to see things more clearly. Officer Weaver seemed to understand. She said to take it easy, watching Estelle all the way to her car. Then Estelle found herself driving home under a bright full moon. If her husband was waiting, she started to think—but she couldn't fill in the rest. He had no reason to be there. His things were almost gone. Even the way he had reacted last week to the news of her interview was deliberately kind. "Good for you!" he had said, cordially. It might have been the way he responded when his students balanced equations. She had seen him write such things at the tops of midterms, when they used to work in bed together and she would read, her head on his chest, his hand idling through her hair.

She pulled in the empty driveway and looked at their house, where all the lights were out. That's when she understood that all her thoughts today—about his waiting, his attending to her— were really just another kind of hope, a way of putting off the fact that he would stop returning, and that she had made him leave. She couldn't remember how to take him in. For some time, she had withdrawn from him in pieces, as if by teaspoon. At first, she withheld the absurdities of the courtroom, things she might have said. Then she withheld her sorrow, her smile, her curiosity. She stopped asking about his day, stopped listening when he spoke. He tried to snap her out of it. "You work every day around people who suffer a thousand times worse than you, Stelle," he said. "They manage to survive." Which was just another way of saying her sadness didn't rank. And which overlooked the fact that those people reappeared until they were incarcerated or done away with otherwise. They embodied the wrong kind perseverance. She mentioned that for a teacher, he should be better at making analogies. It didn't take long to exhaust his empathy. Finally, he tried to rile her. "What are you grieving for after all this time?" he asked on their anniversary, when she sat oblivious to his roses. "They weren't really even children. And if they had been, they might have died in the crib or grown up to be drug dealers or serial killers or worse. People lose teenagers, full-grown kids they've nurtured for years. And here you are, glued to your chair, haunted by ghosts of what? Of what might have been. Of possibility." That night, he began sleeping on the couch.

But she couldn't make herself cooperate. Some nights, she pretended to come down for a book and watched him sleeping, her husband, this good man she was driving away. She was mystified. After everything, he still slept untroubled, as well as he always had. His sleeptalk revealed no secrets, no illicit desires, no rage at lurking bogeymen who spooked and stole and hoarded. He never woke up falling. Instead, he was helpful, teacherly, even in dreams. He mumbled directions to passersby and gave strangers the time. "Pardon me?" he'd say. "Eleven thirty. Mmmm, you're welcome." He said, "I'd be happy to," and "If you don't mind," and "No problem, I'll check." He was decent from skin to marrow.

Which made his moving out all the more wrenching, and irritating. Because he felt guilty about his biggest blow—leaving her—he apologized for smaller things hundreds of times a day. When he bumped her chair, when he left his blankets on the couch. When he over-salted the fish fillets or turned a lamp too bright. Before he threw in the towel and packed it away, they had lived in an efficient present tense, emptied of past and future. He was relentlessly conscientious, and in this way, talk became administration: Did you let the cats in? Feed the cats? Buy the cat food? Have you paid the cable bill? Where is my blue shirt, my wallet, the fabric softener, are you done with the phone, can I take that bookshelf, should I make soup for both of us or should I order pizza?

It was the kind of conversation that articulated their silences. They used to rage about criminals in her courtroom and invent more fitting punishments. They made up songs about their cats and railed about teachers' salaries. They tried to understand Paul's father and argued over landscaping and imagined together the perfect bathtub so they could both fit without squishing. When they were pregnant, they talked about what their baby was doing each day—growing a heart, budding fingers, swallowing.

Walking through the house now, she heard a different kind of quiet. Mail was in the box. The rooms were dark. The cats rolled on the carpet, hungry. She stopped before she came to the living room. All the muscles in her body tensed like violins in tremolo. She knew it before she turned the corner.

The couch was gone.

The carpet held its imprint. Other things were gone—shelves here, a throw rug there—and it looked odd, this room with gaps like missing teeth. It felt brutal as an uppercut, though none of it was sudden or surprising. And yet it was. Now what was she supposed to do? Open some canned food and eat over the sink? Pick up phone messages from Mimi, from her parents, asking about her day? Sob and rage dramatically, slamming doors to empty rooms?

She recognized this moment as the one she'd been putting off all day, perhaps for all her life. It was the minute after something left for good. She had seen it when she was young and her house burned down, a whoosh of heat that collapsed into a giant, smoking puddle. She had seen it in her son, holding him in her arms, as he went from laboring to stay alive to irrevocably dead. His lips opened and turned purple, then white, and his fingers spread and stiffened, like he'd been seized by whatever was the opposite of breath. Failure to thrive—he was the very picture. Before she could cry, before they went home and carted the crib to Goodwill and became strangers to each other, before they returned to the world of muddling through, she inhabited that moment, suspended. She had read stories where someone died in someone's arms, how the body grew heavy, turned to cold flesh without the levity of a spirit. But with her son, it was the opposite. As he died, he grew lighter, as if all the effort it took for him to live had a certain mass. She had tried to put it into words for Paul, talking of burdens lifting, but it sounded hokey and elegiac in the way of greeting cards. Now the room looked lighter, too. Thinned out, less cluttered. No shoes or boxes or dirty clothes. Nothing to stumble on. Nothing to bump into anymore or trip over in the dark.

In a little while, she would write a note explaining this. She would thank everyone for offering her something sweet that, despite her tries, she could not swallow and couldn't grow. She was finished with beginnings. She was so sorry. She would feed the cats and tidy up and lie in the bathtub and leave the doors unlocked. There would be nothing more to do. But for now, she would stay here in this room, sit on the floor and take it in, holding it close to her, holding its weight, its warmth, before it slipped away.

the assignment

"**I** need you to attack me."

Carter's girlfriend Jen said this as she was warming up for aerobics. She sat on the floor with her legs splayed in a way that looked both hot and impossible, stretching over one leg, then the other. At the moment, she was talking to her ankle. Carter wasn't sure he'd heard right. It was a lot to take in at once.

Jen raised her head and slowed it down. "Attack me. Unexpectedly. On the street. Like a bad guy."

Carter looked out the window. They were at her apartment, and over the rooftops, he could see the antennae of the T.V. station where he freelanced camerawork. In a few minutes, he would walk Jen down to the city Y for her class. Jen always seemed to be in motion. She ran five marathons a year, all over the country, in places like Hawaii, New York City, even Disneyworld. That was how they met. He was assigned to film their city's inaugural marathon, and she was the hometown favorite, and as she bounced past each checkpoint—tiny, freckled, sinewy but not stringy, wearing an orange sports bra and her hair in a ponytail—he could focus only on her. So much so that his producer wondered, watching the tape, if any other runners had shown up that day. She had placed second, but told everyone, as she winked at Carter—a woman who winked—that she'd gone home with the real prize. Lately, she was running twenty miles on Saturdays. But last weekend, she had been spooked on a long run through the park. She had been dwelling on it. For his part, Carter was keeping an eye out, escorting her nearly everywhere, installing chains on her doors, staying over.

Still, attacking his girlfriend was a whole other matter. He said, "Jen, haven't you had enough of that already?"

"That's why I want you to do this, Carter. To condition me. In case I need to defend myself, again." She put her legs together and reached over her toes. The other night, he had painted her toenails, the only part of her that seemed to get kind of ugly.

"Can't you take a class or something? I mean, isn't that better?" he asked.

"I'll take a class, sure. They'll tell me how to yell 'No!' really loud. How to carry my keys. Maybe, for the final exam, I'll get to knee someone in the nads."

Her bluntness could surprise him. "They teach you more than that, don't they?" he asked. "Like karate chops or jujitsu?" He did a bad imitation of someone whipping nunchuks.

She shook her head. "The classes around here don't train you in street fighting. They don't ambush you. I need to be ready for something more realistic."

"And it's more realistic for your boyfriend to act like a criminal?"

"I think so."

"You want me to grab you. On the street."

"Yes."

"So you can fight me off."

"Right."

"I can't do that."

"Why not?"

He sat on her couch and tapped his feet on the floor. He tried to imagine sneaking up on her, pouncing. It seemed ridiculous and kinky, like some sex game middle-aged people played with trench coats and handcuffs.

"I just can't," he said. "It's like a porno."

She motioned for him to push on her back to intensify the stretch, as she put it, and so he did. "Carter, not everything is about sex. That's the last thing I'm thinking about. It's the exact opposite."

He stroked her back. "But isn't it weird? To have your own boyfriend attacking you?"

"I don't think so."

"Why not?" he asked.

"Because I trust you. If I make a mistake, it's still okay. And as much as I fight, I know you won't hurt me."

She stood up. He was a whole foot taller, and he secretly thrilled whenever she looked up at him. Her cheeks were ruddy. Her neck and shoulders glistened with sweat, and she smelled musky, heated. Carter leaned low and tasted salt on her ears. Her top was snug as a scuba suit. She stopped his working fingers.

"Carter. Will you help me?"

"I'll think about it," he said, lifting her up, kissing her, her hard little thighs clamped around his waist, the length of her body clenched, like a fist.

He had warned her about running alone through the park, but Jen was older, which gave her the right not to listen. Even after months together, she still teased about their age difference, the way women matured faster. "Think about it," she would say. "You're twenty-six. In male years, that's like nineteen." She was thirty-two and claimed she looked and felt better now than she did at his age. In the pictures around her apartment—at the finish line in Chicago, smiling from a windy mountaintop, arm in arm with roommates at a reunion—she did look puffier in her face, her hair, her baggy clothes. Like the women Carter worked with at the station, age had made her sleek. He liked the fact that her hair was long when so many women sheared it off. Short hair made older women look matronly, or like lesbians, Carter thought. Jen was sprightly and sped through crowds, faster than he could keep up. She taught nutrition as an adjunct at the college, and enjoyed looking just as young as her students. It could be unnerving.

"Joe Linebacker stayed late after class today," she told him once. "I think he wanted to pound my erasers." Lots of athletes took her courses, and Carter could picture them, watching her ass as she wrote on the board, looking down her T-shirts. None of his college teachers had been good-looking. They were, to a person, bearded, quiet, techie types with soft, stained bellies hanging over their jeans. If Jen had been his teacher, he would have been a perfect, obedient, attentive student. And he would never have learned a thing.

She could be charmed by her students because, she told him, they were sweet and awkward and everyone knew that nothing was going to happen. "I don't give off that kind of vibe," she said. "Believe it or not, I'm all business in the classroom." And he believed her, since she tended to be all business in every room. Even in the bedroom, where he'd done okay with younger girls, she would nudge errant parts of him into more satisfying places. He would start to feel embarrassed, but then, as she began to moan, he would simply roll with it. Afterward, her body would loosen and she would whisper his name in what he would call gratitude, and he felt accomplished, like he had cracked something open, a walnut maybe, or a code.

But for all the quarterbacks who asked for help with their papers, for all the goalies who lingered, copying notes, nothing had unnerved her like her last long run. Usually, she ran with a partner, or early in the morning; daylight and crowds offered the illusion of safety. On Saturday, she had made the mistake of heading out in the afternoon for a long run. At the time, Carter was working his other job, shooting low-budget commercials. She had paged him and when he reached her, she was crying. He had never seen Jen cry. It rattled him, even though she said it was just a close call. A thing you might not even tell the police.

She had been running through the city park. Dusk was falling when she rounded the overlook, the part of the park where men sat alone in their cars, jerking off, toking up, waiting for something to fix their eyes on—the sunset or young boys or a pretty girl jogging by. Jen realized too late that no one else was around. Just three cars, curbed, a lone man at each wheel. She ran in the middle of the street, between the parked weirdos and the shadowy undergrowth, where she always said it was a matter of time before someone found a body. Out of one window, a man's voice called, "Hey, honey." Jen glimpsed a pale face, shoulders working frantically. She sprinted away. Fast as she could, she ran down the hill, towards the fountain where families strolled, throwing pennies. But headlights followed her, matching her pace. For a long stretch, she ran alone in the glare. The car sped ahead of her and pulled over and the driver cut the lights. She jumped off the sidewalk, into the woods, as a car door slammed. The man made his way into the brambles and called, "Now, honey. Where'd you get to?" She couldn't see where to put her feet, so she froze behind a tree.

Then, in a voice so close she swore she smelled muscatel, the man said, "Oh, there you are." Behind her, branches snapped. A hand grabbed her by the ponytail and Jen couldn't even scream. Her head snapped as he pulled her back, as she reached for branches, trees, until a voice from the sidewalk called, "Hey, buddy! Is this your car?" In that moment, she tore free. She slid down an embankment and leapt through a hedge, scratching her cheeks, snagging her clothes. She reached the fountain and doubled over for air. Two women pushing strollers asked if she was okay. When she looked back, the man was gone. The women walked her to her car, and she drove home.

They talked about filing a police report, but it was useless. Jen was a terrible witness. She couldn't remember the color or make of the car; all she could summon about the man was "White. Male. Creepy. Diligent." She seemed embarrassed about remembering so little, about being made to feel so small. For Jen, defeat was something you calibrated through carbohydrates, attitude, breath. Only after struggling for minutes would she hand Carter the things she couldn't open.

She didn't want him to fuss over her, and for the most part, he complied. But away from her, as he thought about what had happened, he found himself cruising the overlook, sometimes stopping there. He was tall and thin and had been in a fight only once, in high school, when a meathead senior dropped him in one blow. But the kind of guy who would attack a woman like Jen had to be spineless, measly. Even if he carried a gun, Carter held the element of surprise. He would be patient and ruthless. He tried to imagine how it might play out. How to approach: to casually ask for a cigarette then pound the guy, or drive him off the road, or catch him in the act with his next quivering victim. When he forced the guy to his knees, Carter imagined saying something coolly menacing, crisp: *You have dishonored my family,* or *Feel lucky, punk?* He had a hard time imagining what might come next, or more precisely, his role in the conflict. He wasn't particularly quick or savage or agile or good with weapons; he was merely righteous. It gave him a story to think about as he lurked around the overlook. And so for awhile, until Jen insisted that he hunt her instead, he spent hours in the park, alone, at the curb, waiting for a pretty girl to jog by, ready to punish whoever might follow.

When he wasn't cruising the park, Carter spent his time filming late-night television commercials, the kind where people suffered absurd miseries with everyday appliances, but through whatever was being advertised, restored their lives to grace and efficiency. The ads had two parts: the clumsy labor of before, and the smiling ease of after. In the befores, Carter's job was to capture the hassle of ordinary products. Right now, they were filming a before for a product called The Slice Wizard. A pretty blonde named Charity was demonstrating the frustrations of chopping with everyday cutlery. Carter zoomed in on Charity's hands as they flopped over vegetables, stabbing ineptly. Ragged chunks of red pepper went flying. Charity was a pro. You'd think the invention of knives was a total failure.

"More exasperation, darling," called Elonzo, the director, who had shot five years' worth of befores and afters but insisted these commercials were merely a steppingstone. "Charity, you must emote with your fingers."

"How's this?" asked Charity, extending her middle finger. "Can you sense what I'm feeling now?"

Unlike Elonzo, Charity had no illusions about her career. She was happy for clean work of any kind. She had been a teenage runaway who was lured into porn, inhaled tons of coke, got arrested, then married her parole officer. When she wasn't tumbling out of dangerous ordinary wading pools, or flipping gloppy pancakes with time-consuming standard spatulas, or writhing on lumpy regular air mattresses, she was a phlebotomist at a clinic down the street. She was forthright and honest, and had even told Carter, because he couldn't help asking, about her days in porn. She didn't remember much about it. For an actress, she said, porn and appliance commercials were pretty much the same. You acted pent up before and elated after. You spent a lot of time on what happened between. Satisfaction and relief were always the goals. Appliances could lead to unimaginable ecstasy.

Charity was hard-bitten and worldly and offered practical advice. And lately, everything solid in Carter's life seemed to be teetering. Weeks after the incident in the park, Jen was crying whenever she wasn't barking out some kind of order. It was like she had split into two unrelenting forces—the needy and emotional side which until now, had kept quiet, and the drill sergeant who insisted he floss and eat brown rice and rinse the sink free of stubble. This was the side that also demanded that he attack her, and so on a break, Carter asked Charity what to do.

"Let me get this straight. She wants you to follow and ambush her so she can kick your ass?" Charity picked pepper flesh from her nails.

"That's about it," he said.

She inspected her cuticles. "I knew folks like that."

He nodded. The next scene was supposed to take place in a different kitchen, where another poor loser was to endure the hardships of knives. Elonzo's brother ran a construction business and let them shoot in his display models. Carter watched the gaffer, who was also an actor named Riqué, fiddle with the lights.

"Do you think this experience turned her on?" Charity asked. She brushed vegetable pulp from her tightly stretched sweater. One night, drunk and lonely, before he had met Jen, Carter had rented one of Charity's films. The actress bending and bouncing and sighing onscreen seemed different from the Charity who now filled his lenses—younger, more glazed and vacant somehow—until the camera zoomed in for the money shot. Her mouth was unmistakable. Thinking about it sometimes made Carter fumble as he loaded film, as he was doing now.

He answered, "Turned on? Ha. No way. That department is a whole other subject."

"Well, seriously, Carter, Jen's been rattled," Charity said. "A woman like her is used to being tough." She lowered her voice and looked around. "Take it from someone who's been there: after a thing like that, where you feel overpowered, you won't ever be at someone's mercy again."

Carter stopped loading the camera. "You—?"

They stood shoulder to shoulder. Charity raised her chin to his ear and whispered, "There were shithead directors, back when I was a kid. They forced you to 'audition.' It was porn. You couldn't exactly call 911."

His mind worked to reconcile several things at once: an image of Charity as a kid, scared, pinned down by some fat sleazebag; her supple mouth; and how close she was now, her hot breath in his ear, the smell of red peppers and honeysuckle perfume.

"If you tell anybody, I'll tear you up." She took his hand and wrapped it around her waist, causing a thin sweat to break out on his nose. Her breasts pressed into him. At the back of her waistband, his fingers hit something hard. It was a gun. A small, almost invisible, almost dainty, gun.

"Like the Boy Scouts say," she told him.

Carter was stunned. He didn't know how to respond. All the months they'd been working together, Charity could have shot him. Every time they'd shared a sandwich or bitched about Elonzo or made fun of Riqué's hair, all the times he had trusted her with his secrets, she was waiting for one false move. She could turn that fast. It was disappointing and confusing. It was just another example of how trouble hid itself inside the warmest, brightest places. Without warning a shadow would clear, exposing tender, ugly things, like pillbugs that scattered when you lifted a log.

"Help her out, Carter," Charity said in his ear. "Be kind. Give her time. She'll come around."

She sat back and flashed her actress smile again, the slick, fake charm of after.

So Carter put off Jen's request for a few more weeks, attending to her in other ways. He brought over combat movies: stories of fierce, vengeful women, or dubbed kung-fu films with spin-kicks and grunts. Jen liked the one from Hong Kong with a blind girl, a hitman, and a cop in pursuit, and hundreds of slow-motion flapping doves. When the hitman was struck in the eyes, and he and the blind girl crawled through the carnage, searching, missing each other, Jen welled up with tears. "It's so true," she said, blowing her nose. "Love is exactly like that." As usual, Carter was mystified. Was she talking about him or the boyfriends she had lived with—the fiancé who'd left to aid refugees, the climber who'd vanished into a mountainside crack? If she was talking about them, to him, should he be offended? He never could tell if she was being playful or mean. Sometimes she seemed to change meanings as she talked, saying, "I'm kidding," or "Don't be so sensitive," or, worst of all, "Young people." He was the kind of guy who took teasing to heart and never came back with the perfect line, even later.

Since the incident in the park, though, he occasionally got to lead. Now he was finally getting to watch the movies *he* liked, the kind he hoped to shoot some day on a fiery Hollywood soundstage. Carter aspired to shoot big budget action. There was artistry in violence if you framed it right. One night, he explained this to Jen, as they watched a classic, *Enter the Dragon*. She didn't mind, lately, when he talked over the dialogue, explaining the errors and brilliance of certain shots.

Onscreen, the woman playing Bruce Lee's sister was running from a gang of thugs. Over bridges, through shacks, fleeing by an ankle-length, a knuckle.

"See how the camera is perched above her?" he asked, like a professor. "They're shooting from a crane, which makes her look smaller, more helpless. It heightens the suspense."

"Mmmmmm," Jen said, absorbed.

The woman onscreen ran into a shack. The camera panned to the bright opaque windows, blocked by broken furniture. "And here," he said. "See how the windows look white? Like escape is clear and so close, and yet so far." The thugs broke through the windows and surrounded the woman, who sank to the floor. Her eyes, in a close-up, flashed defeat, then defiance. The woman grabbed a shard of window glass, plunged it deep into her own gut, and died. The picture dissolved. It was an excellent scene.

Jen sat in the darkness, contemplative, quiet. Carter felt learned, sharp. His girlfriend seemed to be watching through the lens he had described, his lens, how he might compose a scene. At that moment, he knew they were seeing things in the same way, their eyes moving over the screen, synchronized. He imagined their brains flashing simultaneously, connected by sizzling branches of lightning, as actors whirled and collapsed in a heap. Something crackled through him. He fell silent for a long time, not wanting to break the circuit.

He waited until the best scene of all, when Bruce Lee chased the villain through a hall of mirrors. He wanted her to understand how, in typical hall-of-mirrors scenes, the villain's presence was inescapable, reflected on every surface—but this scene was better. It was composed of glimpses: a hand appeared as hundreds of hands, always slipping out of view. The hero's face, the villain's shoulder, each vanished into light. You almost never saw the whole.

But when he turned to look at her, she was asleep. When he woke her, she smiled and patted his hand. "That was really great."

Irritated, he refilled his beer in the kitchen.

"So when are you going attack me?" Jen called. "I need to practice. I can't learn just by watching."

Walking in, he remembered how Charity had said to be patient, so he controlled his tone. "I don't want to attack you, Jen. I've told you a million times."

"Come on."

"No."

"Well then," she said, after awhile. "Maybe I can get one of my students to do it."

It was a bluff, Carter thought. At the same time, she'd told him that between boyfriends, she had asked students for other kinds of help—moving bookcases, apartment-sitting, rides to the airport. One schmoe had even carted her all around town to look at new cars after her Honda had been totaled. "I hope he got an A," Carter had smirked. "You bet he did," she'd replied, and winked.

Now he said, with surprising coldness, "Fine, do that. Maybe you should ask someone you gave a C to. Let him chase you down and act out his fantasies of revenge."

She made a sound in the back of her throat like the wind had been knocked out of her. "I can't believe you just said that, Carter.

Don't you know how scary it is to think someone *wanted* to hurt me? That someone, in his sick way, thought that I *deserved* it? That he chased me down so he could make me scream and bleed and beg—" She started to cry. Again.

He put his arms around her, feeling a thousand things at once. Vengeance against the freak who had messed things up between them. Sadness for something huge Jen had lost and seemed, constantly, to mourn. Frailty at his failures, for being weak, for giving in. The low blue flame of stifled anger. And another feeling, a queasiness, the roll and pitch of being unmoored. It wasn't unfamiliar.

"I'll help you Jen," he said, knowing it was the right thing to say. Knowing, as well, it was the completely wrong thing to do.

There was a time, years before, during college, when Carter had followed another girl—a girlfriend who had dumped him in a rush, without warning. He had been young and very confused. For weeks, he couldn't eat or focus on school. Mostly, he'd lain in bed with the radio on, feeling heavy and empty, like a deflated raft. Since she hadn't explained why, he tried to fill in the blanks. It all started as innocently as that: an attempt to understand, to remedy, to reconcile. For example, maybe he hadn't paid enough attention to her. Maybe she was trying to make him notice how much he needed her. And with each hour that passed without her soft, smooth body and melodious laugh, he was noticing, oh how he noticed, she was gone. All the songs on the radio told him to never let go, to hold on for one more day. His buddies talked about how girls liked to be chased. Girls played games like that. Carter himself had been ignored by many girls who later agreed to go out with him, if only for one time, and then only in a group.

So, he convinced himself that she had broken things off to make a point and was waiting for him to make some dramatic statement. At the time, it seemed almost logical.

He drove past her apartment one night after film class, but her car wasn't there. He pulled onto a side street. In his backseat was a basket filled with champagne, strawberries, whipped cream—all the cheesy stuff from the soap opera she watched and he pretended not to watch with her. It was proof he would never mock her interests again. He spent the next hour imagining how she would open her door and at first, be a little angry—she had been upset when he wouldn't stop calling and when they'd crossed paths on campus—but he knew she would be stunned by his thoughtfulness and surprising good taste. She would welcome him inside and somehow they would end up naked, accidentally rolling over the basket, mashing strawberries into their skins, laughing and licking off the pulp.

But an hour passed, then a few, without her coming home. Her roommate pulled in drunkenly at 2:30 A.M. and stumbled to the door with some last-call score. Carter watched as the girl dropped her keys on the steps and he remembered driving home with his girlfriend, buzzed and happy, sliding his hand up her skirt, into her underwear, as he drove. Where the hell was she? He told himself to relax. She was probably at the sorority house, hugging one of her friends, who always seemed to be starving themselves or getting their hearts broken or disappointing their parents. Maybe she was there, crying over him. Or maybe her car was in the shop, he reasoned, when she wasn't there or anywhere else he could think of. He drove around, looking for her, until the birds chattered awake. At a pancake house, he poked shakily at breakfast until it was time for class. He took notes that splintered off into sleep and squirmed through droning lectures. When he made his way home again, her car was parked, nosing the garage door, revealing nothing.

He learned nothing new the next night, or the next.

But waiting for her had ruptured something that only finding her could heal. On Thursday night, he nodded off and missed the moment when she pulled in. He clearly had to change his life. He would never win her back unless he knew where she went, and he couldn't figure that out without tracking her in the day. To be accurate he kept a notebook, and to be sly he wrote in code. He was aware that some people didn't think that following an ex-girlfriend was logical and necessary, even though it was. And how else could he prove he was better now, and more worthy? How else could he understand what he had lacked and meet her needs? Later, he realized such thinking was a poorly linked chain of cause and effect, like some school project of construction paper and tape, half-torn and cobbled together, impressive only to him and people who loved him anyway. His roommate agreed he deserved some answers. His mother agreed he should improve himself. His dad agreed he had a right to hope. If Carter left out the part where he drove around all night and all day, searching, recording his ex-girlfriend's movements, what he was feeling seemed agreeable to just about everyone.

In this way, he justified a number of obviously bad decisions. Like practicing his lenswork on her front door. Like zooming in on the shadows at her bedroom window. Like throwing a brick through the window one night, when two silhouettes started undressing each other. Like trying to hurdle hedges with a bulky, school-issued news camera. Like fleeing the scene with a squeal of tires, trying to outrace lights and sirens.

He ended up in jail. The police opened his camera and played the tape, one of a series in his car, now impounded. His parents were humiliated posting bail and outraged by attorney's fees. Carter thrummed with rage. He pled to some misdemeanors and consented to counseling, but all the while, he felt coerced. He had no choice but to lick his wounds and transfer schools. After awhile, he met other girls and started feeling better. No one knew how he'd spent that year, and there was no reason to tell. He couldn't be like that anymore. Even if he was driving all around town once again, looking to find a girl he loved, waiting, holding his breath, to catch her.

He would attack her sometime during the week. Jen gave him a copy of her schedule, down to clothes she planned to wear. This wasn't only for his benefit. She had started recording her where-abouts down to the smallest detail in case she suddenly went missing; she didn't want her Last Seen Wearing and Last Seen At to be misreported. Carter thought it was overkill but kept his mouth shut, as was now his habit. He seemed to exist to be denied. When he woke in her bed, enfolding her, his hands filling her deep warm crevices and roaming her hard rises, he could only hope she'd stay half-asleep enough to take him in. Then, she was pliant, unsuspecting, dreamy, untroubled by headaches or things to do. She had him constantly lying in wait.

But he wouldn't do everything she said. For one, he wouldn't wear a mask. He'd find other means of disguise. Digging through drawers at his apartment, he threw on some flannel shirts and a college sweatshirt. He unearthed a pair of hulking skinhead boots, leftover, he guessed, from a roommate. The final touch would be a hat. He bought a knit wool cap at the Salvation Army, and at the store, as weary mothers picked through children's shoes, Carter checked himself out. The mirror was kid-sized, and he could only see himself in parts—heavy boots, padded pants, hands flexing in salvaged gloves. Ducking, he could see his chest looked huge, almost soft, but the hat was a whole other matter.

Pulled low, it made him look like a hip young actor incognito. In pieces, anyway, he appeared gritty. Nothing like his normal self.

He examined Jen's itinerary. She was supposed to be on campus for the next few hours. He pulled into the main parking lot and located her car, but scanning the lot, as security trucks drove steadily by, he saw his attack being thwarted by good Samaritans. With his record, he had to be careful.

Aimless, he pulled into a spot and watched the change of classes. Girls dressed up on this campus, wearing tight black pants and sweaters without bras, nipples sharp, jiggling, laughing. The kind of girls who would have ignored him in college, but who might find an older man intriguing. No one knew him here. Sitting low, his car among rows and rows of cars, he felt powerful in his anonymity, a stranger, a bad guy, and he let his mind drift into corners that Carter never would. He didn't have to watch and simply frame the action; he could be a player. He watched a bouncy blond crouch to tie her shoe and pictured himself standing before her, her face rising up, smiling, confused, as he grabbed her head, cradling her skull. Her small bright head in his large hands, easily pushed to where he wanted. Usually, his fantasies involved surprising compliance: buttons popping, skirts flying, voices rising, crying, *yes*. But in this scene, holding the girl's head down, forcing her to unzip him, he felt something startling as he imagined her voice, pleading, saying *no*—a feeling he recognized as if from a distance: pleasure.

If he could be anyone, the girl could be anyone, and he let his thoughts stretch—that's what it felt like, stretching—into darker, weirder shapes. The girl's mouth took him in, became Charity's mouth, his hands holding Charity's head, holding Charity's gun. *Tear me up, you say?* he might ask, enjoying the pull as she shook her head. *You're not the only one packing heat.* Looking down on her, her pretty head working, he could let himself be greedy,

taking as he pleased. He wouldn't have to arouse or ply or reci-
procate. He could finally be free.

It was getting too hot to stay in the lot, people milling everywhere. But by the time he maneuvered out of the parking lot,
stopping, slowing, stopping again for clusters of students, he felt
restless, tight. He drove by the display home where they were to
finish the Slice Wizard shoot that night, but thinking of Charity,
he was overcome with repulsion. He felt addled. He passed by
Jen's campus once again, then headed home and paced his small
apartment. He called in sick to the evening shoot. He ate an old
pack of ramen noodles and watched the local news.

When Jen called, wondering if he was coming over, she said,
almost flirtatiously, "I thought I saw you in the lot today. Were
you planning an attack?"

He told her what he thought and hoped and intended to be
true. "No, that wasn't me you saw. It couldn't have been me."

Of course, his apartment's sounds were strange to him now, of
course he couldn't fall asleep, of course he lay awake all night pent
up and irritated. He watched *The Wild Bunch* and *The French
Connection*—for him, comfort films—and drank the only liquid
left in his refrigerator, seven cans of Coors. At dawn, he showered
and looked over Jen's itinerary. She would be at the track. He
dressed in his bad-guy clothes and tried to envision the attack the
way Jen would—without desire, without anger or shame, but as
something clean, athletic. As something more like sport.

Near the track, he parked on a side street and walked to find
Jen's car, one of the few cars in the lot. He ducked behind the
bleachers and watched her through the risers. She was leaning

against the fence, stretching out her calves. She was alone, dressed as she had noted on her schedule: blue tights and a yellow shirt. Carter yearned for her. He missed the way she poked his ribs and argued with the newspaper. He missed picking her up, her tiny fists pounding him, whirling her around until she laughed, and he missed the way her lips turned purple and clung to his after just one glass of red wine. He missed her ropy legs around him and the pride he felt when she took his arm on the sidewalk. He missed her voice, the way it lilted in affection as she called, "Hey there, handsome."

"Hey, yourself," a man's voice answered.

Carter rubbed his eyes. Through the bleachers, he saw a muscular man, unseasonably tan, walk up and slap Jen's hand. It had to be some random runner guy. This wasn't on her schedule.

The man had silvery buzz-cut hair and wore microscopic runner shorts—effeminate, Carter thought, probably had a built-in panty. His thighs were chiseled like an Olympic statue, smooth and shiny, despite the chill. Carter stifled his anxiety by imagining the man with a little pink razor, twisting to shave his legs. Jen would chat with him for a minute like any acquaintance and the man would sprint away.

But the man removed his shirt to reveal an equally mighty chest. "You ready to get a little hot?" he asked.

"Hot for you," Jen said, with a laugh.

They began running, slowly at first, round and round, talking the whole time. He worked to make out their words. There seemed to be a lot of teacher talk, and Carter wondered if this guy was a professor, or worse, some kind of coach. Maybe they'd trained together for years, or maybe just since the city marathon. They ran and ran. After hours of watching them loop the track, Carter's eyelids were growing heavy. Maybe what they had was simply banter, shoptalk, like him and Charity. But beneath the talk, there was a current—sneaking, electric, dangerous.

Then Carter heard someone say his name. He strained to listen. He could only make out words like "fine" and "child" and "exhausting." As they passed by the bleachers, he swore he heard Jen say "over," and he held himself utterly still. She said it again. Over. As in staying or not staying overnight, or as in breaking up, or as in finishing their run, as they were doing now?

He stood frozen, processing. Did she think of him like one of her students? Like some dumb sweet freshman who dallied in her company—someone to pass along? All at once, he saw their lives together in two ways, framed side by side, like a before and after—except he hadn't seen the before part so clearly until he was here, in the after. He could see that before the park incident, before right now, he had hoped they would last forever. Her focus had lifted him, threaded him with a sense of direction, gave him the feeling he could hurdle anything. It was cheesy, but he had always envisioned them arm in arm, crossing a finish line. He understood it now from the perspective of something he had lost, the way Jen might have seen the winner's podium at the marathon, as she stood in second place.

In the after, though, he saw himself as one in a series—one lap around the track maybe, a single frame on the reel of her life. The boyfriend Carter would fade out, and the next guy would appear: silver-haired, virile, oaken. Here he was, a dreamy kid obsessed with car chases, ninjas, breasts. Look how she had him standing here, in costume, like a child at Halloween. She was diminishing him and would keep it up until he was a speck against the landscape.

He walked to his car. He drove to her apartment building and hid his car in an alley and scaled the stairs of the fire exit. The back window broke easily beneath his fists, his hands protected in their gloves. He crashed over the glass in his clunky boots, and stepped through her apartment. He looked around. His presence barely registered here; he didn't even have a drawer. Good. The fewer pieces that existed—scattered clothes, a borrowed tooth-brush—the more easily he could vanish.

He arranged himself and waited. He pictured her climbing the shadowy stairs, toweling her face, pulling off her shirt, wan-dering, winded, in her little orange sports bra to her ordinary, everyday front door. He imagined looking down on both of them, as if from a great height. In this way, he could watch—her, tiny, unsuspecting, on one side of her door, a stranger crouching on the other—two halves that once seemed to fit together the way a key turns in a lock. He took a deep breath that felt like laughter. Something was about to turn all right. After all, she had asked for it.

worship for shut-ins

It isn't really the pain that sticks, or the car careening towards her, or the slow, horrific realization that no one is at the wheel. It is the sound of the impact that Valerie can't shake: the startled yelp of her dog Cass being hit, then crushed to death. At night, when she falls into a drugged netherworld between sleep and misery, as she tries to curb her habit of rolling onto her side—now swollen, grillwork branded on her thigh—the sound of her dying dog finds its way into every dream. It becomes the sound of a chair scraping the floor in her childhood home, the creak of an attic door, the sob of her ex-husband collapsing when she packed her things and left. It's the sound of her mother falling, surprised, through the floorboards when Valerie was six, the sound of terrors still at large: her brother gasping beneath his kayak, her father arresting in heart attack. The dreams begin in sun and color, like the day she walked her dog, when lilacs bloomed and grass grew high—spring in southern Ohio. Then, like the accident, she turns a corner into the path of a shattering blow. She stands helpless against the pull of water, of gravity. Before she wakes, everyone cries out to her—an ugly, baffled sound—and Valerie can only listen.

Her waking hours are just the opposite, silent as empty pockets. The mornings are quiet when Cass should rattle her tags; the floors are still. No one watches over her small apartment, discerning threat in noises, and Valerie is a bumbling keeper, shaky as Barney Fife. With one exception—when the dog fell mysteriously ill this winter and had to be hospitalized—Cass had been with her every day for seven years. After the divorce, when Valerie started buying wine in gallon cartons, Cass was excellent company. The dog sat close as Valerie watched T.V. and rode shotgun on scenic drives, and out of gratitude, Valerie would walk her through the pet store, letting her sneak bones. Wherever Valerie took the dog, people stopped to talk. They asked about Cass's spotted tongue, her tail curled like a question mark. In this way, Cass eased Valerie's awkwardness, made her seem approachable: a person with anecdotes, amusing facts, a dog that barked on cue. On weekends, when the starkness of her life grew sharp and there was nothing to do but drink, Cass walked up and raised her head—a warm place to rest a hand.

And so Valerie starts whenever something taps in the hallway, the sound of nails on a linoleum floor. She sits up too fast and moans: today, it's the metal mail chute flapping. She is propped up on the couch, immobile, the things she needs—Percoset, the box of Beaujolais—in easy reach. But when it comes to anything else, Valerie has to wait for her brother, James. Before the accident, when James would pull into the driveway, Cass would bark, fangs bared, spit flying, and he would open the door and shout, "Well, if this hound is Cerebus, I must be in hell." James lives downtown, teaches classics at the university, and openly disdains the corporate sprawl of Valerie's suburban neighborhood. He comments on the supermarket chains like a bemused foreigner. "I saw something called a 'hyperstore' as I pulled off the exit," he might say. "What's the difference between that and a 'megastore'? More caffeine? Less Ritalin?" If her brother drives her crazy after twenty minutes, Valerie wonders about his students—if they find him witty and smirk along, or simply pass the time by doodling. It's easy to imagine James as a caricature, in his square-framed hipster glasses, finger raised, a balloon over his head exclaiming, "Culture! It's more than a test!"

But he is her closest relative, good-hearted if predictable, and he stops by every day with urban take-out food. James has a knack for caretaking. He was twelve when their mother fell while laying insulation, hurtling through the attic floorboards, landing on her head. Valerie had been playing in her room when her mother crashed through the ceiling. She had just learned the expression "raining cats and dogs," so a person falling from the sky held a certain charm. Like the cats and dogs that, James had assured her, landed on their feet, Valerie fully expected her mother to dust herself off and begin frolicking in the yard. Except her mother went into seizures. James somehow knew to clear a path and keep their mother's teeth from severing her tongue, and long after their father put Mom in a home, James remains focused where Valerie simply gapes. It makes sense that James is a professor while Valerie, at thirty-five, works a teenager's job. Worked. She doubts she has a job anymore, and doesn't really care. She is sick of the chain café where she runs orders: the endless shriek of the espresso machine, her pierced and snarky manager, steamed milk reeking like baby vomit, coffee grounds beneath her nails.

She pops another pill and washes it down with wine. It's been a while since she's been wasted this early in the day. Until her brother comes to check on her, there isn't much to do. So she works the accident like a story problem, something open-ended and contingent, which, as her thoughts grow slow and sticky, blurs fact into a kind of hope. For example, what would have happened if she had looked up sooner, if she had seen the car was driverless? If she'd let Cass lead at her own pace on their walk, instead of dragging the dog behind her? If she'd let the dog sniff and lollygag? If an idiot kid had remembered to pull his emergency brake as he parked on the hill? If it had been raining?

"You can't keep dwelling on it, Val," James says when he arrives with Indian food, noting Valerie's half-closed, bloodshot eyes. Her stomach growls at the smell of curry and she reaches, or tries to reach, for the food. Her arms seem to be asleep.

Her brother shakes his head. He caps the vial and tosses the empty wine box. "What are you, a rock star?" he admonishes. "Sit up, for Christ's sake. Drink some water."

Valerie obeys. She feels like she hasn't moved in days. Uselessness has spread from her broken left side to the entire rest of her body. It seems both funny and terribly sad that her brother is cutting her food into bites.

"Open up, moron," he says, not unkindly.

She chews. He puts the fork in her good hand, and she steers food into her mouth. Her brother looks tired, and it strikes her— quietly, and in slow motion—that the past week has been stressful for James, that he is worried about her, and that she's not helping anything. The next bite is hard to swallow. James picks over his dinner and Valerie can tell he's ruminating.

Finally, he says, "Val, this isn't working out."

For a minute he sounds like her last boyfriend, who said the same thing, on this same couch, and her heart stops in the same way. She has no one else but James. She starts to cry.

"What the—?" James says, astonished. "Valerie. Val. Hey." He touches her shoulder, the way he used to when they were kids and they visited the hospital. Their mother would be lying there in bed, smiling unevenly, trying so hard to speak—and on the way home, Valerie always cried. She was glad when she could finally burst through the hospital doors, glad they stayed for a short time, glad they only visited a few times a year, but her relief was pierced by shame: what kind of person fled her damaged mother, who waited for months just to be held? And James was always the first to hug Mom, talking to her in a normal voice, full of warmth and information, nothing like the sappy voices of her mother's nurses, who treated everyone like babies.

Without realizing it, she's sunk into her brother's chest—they haven't been this close in years. But she feels so hazy and sore and lost about everything. Or maybe it's just that everything seems lost.

James pats her head and says, "Listen, you have to come home with me. I can't keep this schedule up, and frankly, you're a mess."

Fine, she thinks, nodding, closing her eyes. She hears a flurry of activity as lights are set and things are packed and trash is bagged, taken out. She seems to be floating, then lands abruptly in her wrecked body, in James's passenger seat. All she knows is that she's going somewhere with her brother, windows down, breeze blowing, feeling lighter, bubbly, unsettled, riding from home to home.

Two weeks later, her leg is something to behold. The swelling has subsided and in its place, bruises have bloomed spectacularly—purples, indigos, greens. Since James has no cable and his videos all have subtitles, Valerie watches her body like the weather. Even sober—James rations her pills and allows only supervised visits with wine, good wine, from bottles—she is fascinated, and when her brother returns from campus, she shows off each new explosion.

"Check this out," she says, carefully turning her hip. "I think it's the face of Jesus."

James doesn't look, but seems relieved to find her in good spirits. "At least you have a hobby now," he says. "A better hobby, anyway."

And she's developed other better hobbies. Some days, she talks about the accident with an attorney friend of their father's, and when he isn't in the courtroom, their father calls, too. Dad is a Superior Court justice in their hometown of Columbus, a stoic, righteous man who, in a certain light and depending on Valerie's mood, reminds her of Gregory Peck. Talking to him lately has been almost pleasant: her brush with death has reminded everyone that she still matters, and it has proven that some calamities in her life aren't entirely her fault.

Talking to James has been even better. When they used to drive home for the holidays, conversation was bickering—nothing like the talks they have now when James comes home, before he retreats to his study. Watching him from the other room—typing his manuscript, whooping at student papers—Valerie is surprised. She has only known him from the outside, from her seat in the audience at his graduations, the slight lift in their father's voice when he talks about James's books. But seeing her brother at home—ironing chinos, heating soup, rushing around wet-haired—she feels tender, inspired. He has chosen to keep her close to him, and this makes her feel like giving. For once, Valerie wants to accomplish something. She wants to make someone proud. So she makes a project of walking, trying to maneuver around James's beautiful Victorian apartment, through its pocket doors, over the gleaming hardwood floors, with a cane, toe-splints, and hand-cast.

Every once in a while, she stops to listen to the clamor from upstairs. The people up there are always thundering. Sometimes, as they eat dinner together and something thunks or skitters above, James looks to the ceiling and shouts, "Easy does it, Leadfoot!" The woman upstairs is a nurse, he says—she has a nurse's brisk, heavy stride—and from the sounds of running and growling, she owns about thirty cats.

Which, as she thinks about James's cats, Valerie can't imagine. Hector and Paris are their names but they don't seem to know it. "The cats are assholes," James has warned, but until now, she's never really seen them. The few times she visited in the past, she had business downtown—court dates, a job selling sunglasses on the skywalk. The last time she was here was in winter. She had just dropped off a feverish Cass at an emergency clinic. No one knew what was wrong with her dog, who, suddenly and without warning, couldn't walk or grow white blood cells. She buzzed James from his lobby, sniffling, sick with a panic that now seems quaint: that despite her best efforts, Cass would die, before Valerie was ready. Then, she didn't know where else to go. But James had professor friends over, and the encounter was strange and clumsy. Valerie sat on the couch, unshowered, covered in Cass's hair. No one had anything in common. They all sat swirling snifters.

Finally, a woman with a flippy haircut and leather boots who looked about Valerie's age asked, "So what was your dog's name?"

"Is," Valerie corrected. "Her name is Cass. It's short for Cassidy."

"Really?" asked a younger man in spectacles. "As in Neal?"

"Butch?" someone else asked.

"Shawn!" the woman said, and everybody laughed. Someone started singing and the woman yammered about her teenage crushes, which happened to be the same as Valerie's crushes, but that was beside the point. What kind of arrogant jerks made fun of someone's dying dog? No wonder she'd hated college. She had dropped out to follow the Grateful Dead; her dog was named for their best song.

Now, as she lumbers around the apartment rattling a bag of treats, lonely for a furry touch, the cats arch and hiss and flee. They only creep out when Valerie is asleep on the couch, staring, sniffing her wounds. They swat Valerie's things from the coffee table and hide toys in the toes of her slippers and eat the house-plants, then fill the halls with the sound and spill of puking.

So it is with some reservation that she agrees to cat-sit for her brother. The quarter is ending, which means James will leave for his annual month-long trek through Alaska. James believes it is the perfect arrangement.

"It's low maintenance, Val. The easiest job you'll ever have," he says, testing the straps on his backpack. He smiles. "And given your work experience, that's really saying a lot."

Valerie feels grateful and resentful and pitied, all at once. Cat-sitting is not how she wants to prove herself. But she wants to help and do it well, which makes her worry. "You know I'm not 100 percent," she says. "What if I fall and can't get up?" She pictures herself writhing on the floor, the cats throwing up in her hair.

James unearths another bag from the hall closet. He spreads a tent on the living room floor and inspects zippers, seams. "A, that's not going to happen. B, if it does, you have my pager. C, I'll call when I can." As he clicks the tent poles into shape, the cats sidle over, curious.

"But what if I miss your call?" she asks. "What if I'm dead, or out? Or both?"

"Val, please. Where would you go?"

He has her there. He has forwarded her mail, paid her rent, driven her to the doctor, stocked the refrigerator, and programmed the phone with delivery numbers. "Honestly," James says. "Would you rather be back in your place?" Meaning her small, dark, quiet, ugly McApartment far away, with generic neighbors who always forgot her name and mated by the pool.

Her brother clips nylon to the poles and the tent mushrooms to life. The bigger cat, Paris, chews a toggle. James crawls inside the tent, followed by little Hector.

"I wish you could come in here, Val," he calls. "Remember camping in the meadow?"

Valerie lies on the couch, hurting in several places, knowing she couldn't follow him if she tried. Inside the tent, her brother laughs. He fools around with a flashlight and zips and unzips the window flaps, giddy in the little world he's made—the one just outside of hers.

By the time James loads his kayak into an airport van, Valerie is able to twist a can opener and stoop, painfully, to change a litter-box. She can hobble to the lobby to collect the Sunday *Times*. She is able to sit on the balcony and listen as James's neighbors come and go, as they tend to their flower boxes and say hello, talking of heat waves and cold snaps. Whenever she opens the balcony door, Hector and Paris yowl until she lets them out, and for a few minutes, as the cats roll and stretch in the sunlight, Valerie almost likes them. But then they fight each other for the warmest spot and hiss when a door slams, pawing at the screen until she lets them in again. "Pussies," Valerie chides.

Even though she could make her way outside, she stays in James's building. Truth is, she can't leave home. Since James is gone, the pills are gone, and the wine is out of her reach, the accident has taken hold of her with unexpected force. It seems impossible that one minute she was walking, looking up a hill, cursing at what she thought was a reckless driver—and the next, lying on the pavement, mangled, holding a broken leash. That fast. Some days, she is seized by a fit of shaking that frays her aching, knitting parts. Her mind is unraveling, too. For one thing, she can't sleep. She lies on the couch, listening to the occasional thunk from above, the ongoing argument upstairs. Valerie remembers her own awful marriage, fighting with her husband, an explosive, self-reproachful man who liked to throw things, too. The woman upstairs yells just like Valerie, though she can't make out the words: the tone is indignant, exasperated, a one-sided shouting match. Valerie turns up the T.V. She starts watching T.V. until sunrise, watches anything just for company, even the sappy Sunday morning shows for elderly folks who can't make it to church. For people in wheelchairs who stare through the glass at pious cartoon creatures and Oral Roberts. For bed-ridden peo-ple whose nurses tune the channel to "Worship for Shut-Ins," with its cheerless singing and that slap of a title, matching hope to its denial. Shows for people like her mother.

And she is kept awake by a secret, nagging thought: that she might have, could have saved her dog. After all, she had worked so hard when Cass fell sick this winter. But the day Cass died, Valerie hated her dog, the bloated, stinking mess of her. When Cass's illness this winter almost killed her, all that could save her were massive doses of steroids. Valerie was elated, until the drugs took hold. Within months, Cass packed on twenty pounds. She grew ravenous, round, and bad, became a hulking beast, all appetite. The dog shredded trash and soiled the carpets, hoovered the kitchen for specks and crumbs. It was absurdly cruel, how Valerie acted out, calling Cass names like "fatty" and "lard-ass," how, instead of throwing treats for the dog to fetch, she sometimes hurled them at Cass's body, that beach ball with fur and legs. How sometimes, when the dog stood in a doorway—enormous, panting, stupid—Valerie nudged her with her foot, hard: not quite a kick.

All Cass could do was need, need, need. Valerie felt cursed. She had prayed, actually prayed, so hard for Cass to live, and now that she thrived, Valerie was murderous. She wasn't a religious person, so she figured her dog's salvation was punishment for her cheap and selfish faith. After all, what she really wanted was an end to her own suffering; she didn't want to be alone. It was like a story she had read as a child, in which a grieving family wished their dead son back to life with a magic charm. The mother was desperate for her son's return, but the father knew better. There was a knock at the door and on the other side, the father knew, stood a ghoul in the shape of their boy. The father understood his son's return from death would bleed all goodness from the living. He knew that it was wrong to cling to something pure past the point of decency. He had no choice: he wished his son away. And who could blame him? Would anyone really have expected him to care for such a thing?

As she collects James's mail from the box one day, Valerie hears a conversation. On the stairway, a woman is telling a story about an accident, a man thrown from his car. The woman talks in medicalese, but the case boils down to broken arms and broken legs. The amazing thing, the woman says, was how the man survived. He had just finished hiking in a nearby forest and swerved to miss a deer. He waited in shock until the sunlight dimmed, but no one came to his rescue. So this broken, bloodied man felt around for a stick, pulled himself up, dragged himself to the car, positioned himself in the driver's seat, turned the ignition, and shut the door. With a bone poking through his forearm, he pushed his fractured legs on the gas and brake. Agonizingly, slowly, he steered to the main highway, twenty miles away, where someone pulled over to help. "Thank goodness the car wasn't a stick shift," the woman says.

Valerie looks around the corner to see two women halfway up the steps. One of them is wearing scrubs, and she realizes that this small, curly-haired, fortyish woman must be James's upstairs neighbor. Sure enough, her shoes are white and orthopedic. Her face is kindly, round and pink, and she's carrying bags of cat food, and when she notices Valerie, she gives a little wave.

"Are you the new lady on the first floor?" she asks.

Valerie moves closer and explains about James and his cats. "I'm sorry, I was eavesdropping," she says. "That story was amazing. I was just in an accident, too. I sort of understand how that guy feels."

The women take a few steps down and ask Valerie what happened, and they furrow their brows and shake their heads as she tells her own lesser, weirder drama. She hesitates at first, then realizes they're fascinated. She isn't used to holding attention without her dog.

"Isn't that incredible? Your poor dog," the nurse, Nan, says. She looks at Valerie's bandaged hand. "You seem to be making good progress," she observes.

"I guess," Valerie replies. "It sure seems slow. It doesn't help that the cats won't let me sleep." It seems unneighborly to mention the other racket, the clunks and sobs from the floor above.

Nan laughs. "Tell me about it. We have six cats. Three of them hate the other three. We're—what's it called?—a blended family. Gosh, I hope they don't disturb you."

The other neighbor, a wide-eyed redhead, excuses herself and climbs to the third floor. "Newlywed," Nan whispers. "Her husband looks just like her, you'll see. It's sweet, but also kind of creepy."

"Really?" Valerie asks.

"And wait until you get a load of the guy next door to me," Nan says. "We call him 'The Chest.' He likes to walk around without a shirt, but he's just a bony little guy, almost tubercular. Isn't it always the least attractive men who parade around like that." Her eyes twinkle mischievously. "His wife thinks he's the bees' knees, though. They're pretty frisky. We've seen them from our balcony."

Valerie is thrilled to be drawn into someone's confidence. She wants to inspire Nan's trust, to let her know she understands what it's like when the honeymoon is over. It has been a long time since someone asked for Valerie's advice, opened up, shared secrets. She wants to signal that if Nan needs someone to talk to, she has an excellent set of ears. So she says, "Didn't life used to seem so easy?"

"Gosh, I know," Nan says, wistfully, looking up towards her apartment. "Well, it was good to meet you. If you need anything, remember, I'm a nurse. Here's our number." She writes it down on a receipt. She picks up the cat food bag and smiles, then climbs the stairs with a certain heaviness—perhaps it's dread, Valerie thinks.

That night, Nan's footfalls on the floor above seem quieter and nobody yells. Paris curls against Valerie's good leg, purring, and Hector brings her a toy mouse. She doesn't think about her mother, or ex-husband, or departed dog, doesn't imagine James starving in the wilderness or Dad slipping in the shower. She doesn't stare at the top shelf of the pantry and plot a way to reach the cabernet. She thinks only of how she might help Nan, and then she falls asleep.

She thinks she sees an opening when Nan knocks later that week. The night before, Valerie heard stomping on the floor above, doors slamming, Nan yelling, loud. Now in the doorway, Nan has dark circles under her eyes and her hair hangs in strings. She wears scrub bottoms and a tank top. Her arms are pale but muscular.

"Our central air is on the fritz," Nan says, smiling, setting down a basket. "I thought I'd head to the basement, where it's gross and smelly, but at least it's cooler. Do you have any wash? I figured you're probably still having trouble with the stairs."

Valerie invites Nan inside, and she looks around. "Your brother's place is different than ours. Wall sconces, those are nice. There are so many little details in these apartments. When people move out, I always take a peek."

While Valerie gathers her dirty clothes—embarrassingly few, stiff with grit—Nan tells her about the building. "There's a fourth floor here, an attic that used to be servants' quarters. They had to install locks on the doors last year when a homeless guy moved in. Someone heard a television up there. Just think—going about your daily business with a lunatic in your attic."

Valerie takes the chance. "That's not so far off from my marriage, actually," she says, laughing. "My ex-husband was kind of nuts."

"Gosh," Nan says. "You poor little thing. Your dog and your husband, gone. You've had it so darn *hard*." Her voice has taken on a nursey brightness. Out of habit, Valerie smiles like a shy seven-year-old at the rail of a hospital bed. It takes a minute to try again.

"Well, yes," Valerie says, stripping her pillow and shoving dirty clothes in the case. "It was really hard to leave my husband.

We were only married for two years. A full year of that was fighting."

Nan shakes her head. Her eyes shine with sympathy. Not one glimmer of recognition.

Valerie goes for broke. "You ever been married?"

"Gosh, I wish," Nan says. "My shifts are hard on relationships. Plus I'm taking classes. I want to become a Physician's Assistant. It's tough to find a man who can amuse himself while his woman is busy all the time." She laughs. "I mean, amuse himself in healthy ways."

Is this a clue? Valerie can't tell. Nan hangs the pillowcase over her shoulder like a burglar on T.V.

"Hot okay? Can I do them all together?"

The laundry, she means. Valerie nods, and Nan speeds towards the door. But she stops suddenly, turns around, a shadow across her face. Valerie's heart is ready to flutter open like a pair of wings.

"Wait," Nan says. "Where are the cats? You said there were two Siamese?"

"I think they're hiding," Valerie says. "They take awhile to warm up to strangers."

"Oh," Nan laughs. "That's pretty common." She heads out.

Valerie listens hard through the afternoon but hears nothing out of the ordinary. When she leaves the apartment to get the mail, her clothes are folded in a basket by the door. Nan doesn't knock again. Valerie tries to puzzle it out. What's going on up there? Has she ever heard a man's voice during the fights upstairs? Come to think of it, no. Maybe the boyfriend is long-distance. Or maybe it's not a man in Nan's life, but another woman. Valerie thinks of Nan's tank top, her chiseled, boyish arms. If Nan is a lesbian, maybe she keeps it to herself, a smart move in this conservative city. She guesses nurses are conservative, too, that they might shun poor Nan, and thinking about it, Valerie feels sorry for her lonely, possibly-gay neighbor. But she wants Nan to know she is accepting in all matters of the heart. Besides, she has long suspected James is gay, though living here has turned up nothing. He hides no pornography of any kind; his CD collection runs from jazz to classical and, to her surprise, some Delta blues. The only gray area is his collection of shoes, if stereotypes hold true: James has exquisite taste in footwear—wingtips, tassels, suede, several pairs of clogs.

Of course it's possible, Valerie knows, that Nan could be crazy. Her ex-husband talked to himself, for example. But he talked to calm his temper down, self-counseling, the therapists called it; and when Valerie talks to herself, drunk or sober, it is just to hear a human voice. Only love could drive a person to fight so fiercely, and so often.

She walks into the hallway: she will return the laundry basket to Nan and that will settle everything. She takes a deep breath and climbs the staircase.

The first step is excruciating. The next three are even worse. There is no way to hold the basket in her bandaged hand, no way to raise her leg without nearly fainting, no way that clutching the banister will appease her body's sudden anger. The pain is fresh, astonishing, the kind that lingers to make a point. Valerie is flooded with panic. How will she make it through the night?

The only thing worse than heading up, she realizes, is trying to work her way back down. She can't lower herself to sit and rest; she hurts too badly to crawl. She thinks of the hiker thrown from his car in the woods, pulling his broken body towards relief. If he can do that, she reasons, limping through the door, surely she can use her cane to tap James's cabernet off the pantry shelf. And yes indeed, it hurts like hell, as does the effort of the corkscrew, but after a few glasses, she toasts herself: she is, after all, a survivor.

Two days later, Valerie opens the door and finds cookies and a friendly note: "Rx: The healing power of chocolate. Enjoy, Nan." She hasn't had homemade cookies in forever. She brims with gratitude and simply can't get over her good fortune. Making friends has been such a struggle. Her jobs, generally, aren't staffed with adults or people who care to know her. Among co-workers, she forgets punch lines and whatever gossip she passes along is yesterday's news, and people who aren't very funny to begin with like to complain that she can't take a joke. She tried being open with strangers, once, disastrously, in second grade, when a teacher had Valerie show the class what she'd drawn for the word "quiet." Most kids had sketched bunnies or flying angels or a librarian saying "Shhhh!," but Valerie had crayoned her mom, strapped to the bed so she wouldn't fall out, an X across her mouth. Afterwards, she could have drawn her classmates, her teacher, everyone who stared at her, stunned. But she caught the attention of a freckled boy who had drawn his father's headstone, until the boy changed schools and Valerie fell in with the girls who ate chalk and wore knock-offs of the popular jeans.

But now here is someone who knows she has problems and still leaves her cookies. She realizes she ought to return the favor. She finds Nan's phone number and dials, hearing a faint ringing from above. Nan answers.

"I just wanted to thank you," Valerie says. "The cookies were great."

"Oh! Wonderful," Nan says. "We're chocoholics up here."

"Me, too. Hey, do you like Chinese?" Valerie offers to order delivery this evening when Nan gets home from work. But it seems rude not to invite Nan's other half, whatever that may be.

She says, "I'd be happy to set some extra plates for you two. Do you both drink wine?"

Nan's voice gets quiet and she seems to be speaking inside her hand. "You know, it's probably best if we just do this ourselves."

And what can Valerie say? So she won't meet the trouble-maker in her neighbor's life tonight. It's good enough to share a meal.

When Nan comes over, Valerie has tidied up and set out plates and glasses. They sit on the couch. Nan starts telling har-rowing stories from the hospital. Her eyes alight when Valerie talks about the doctors who took care of her, the inept intern who stabbed and stabbed, trying to find a vein. Valerie makes Nan laugh, and Nan seems relaxed, curling into the pillows on James's couch. They fumble with chopsticks and trade appetizers and crack open fortune cookies.

Nan reads her fortune in a somber, deadpan voice. "'Distance lends enchantment to the view.'" She closes her eyes. "It has been written."

Valerie opens hers. Her fortune is nonsense, a mistranslation. "It says, 'Very soon, and in pleasant company.'"

"What?" Nan asks, and Valerie repeats it.

"No, I mean, what is supposed to happen 'very soon,'" Nan asks, "and 'in pleasant company'?"

"I don't know. With my luck, it would be awful. As in, A meteor will fall from the sky and crush you, very soon—but in pleasant company."

"Valerie!" Nan says, slapping Valerie's good knee. "Geez! That's a terrible point of view! Why not, You will win the lottery very soon, with all your friends around."

"With me, it's more like I'll tumble down the stairs in half an hour, with everybody watching."

Nan shakes her head. "Okay, maybe so. But then maybe some-one will help you stand up and brush the dust off your backside."

Valerie considers this. She looks at James's soft furniture, this kind person, so far away from collisions and emergency rooms, noise and panic. "Or maybe nothing will happen at all," she says. "Maybe I'll just keep on breathing and eating and sitting here, in this nice place."

Nan sighs and smiles. "Amen."

They sit together, quiet. Valerie doesn't force Nan to talk about heartache or volunteer her own. Maybe some friendships aren't about showing wounds, but offering a little peace.

Then as Nan leaves, something strange happens. Gathering the delivery boxes, Valerie drops the bottle of soy sauce, scattering broken glass. She curses, apologizes, then stoops awkwardly, pain splintering through her knee. It takes some time to collect the shards. All the while, Nan stands and watches, does nothing as Valerie stumbles, chatters on as Valerie slices her finger, blood dropping in splats on the floor. In fact, Nan eats a cookie. Chews and watches, never offering a hand or checking the size of the cut, letting Valerie wrap her own finger in napkins, this alleged health care professional. When Nan gets up to go, still talking about some show on cable, the napkins are soggy red. "Do you think I need stitches?" Valerie asks. She feels light-headed. "Oh, you'll live," Nan says. "You shouldn't drink so much." And is gone.

The next evening there is another explosive bout of screaming from above. Someone stomps across the floor, yells, then stomps over to what Valerie thinks is the kitchen. Something large and clattery drops: a stack of dishes. When plates start flying, Valerie knows, the only way out is down, so she sits and waits, intrigued and poised and not a little worried. The stomping starts again. A woman's voice says, clearly, "No!" and "Stop!" There's a long, low string of words: the sound of a cruelly specific curse. Something as big as a kitchen table crashes to the floor, and James's cats go running.

Nan's apartment is quiet for a solid minute. A door slams and there is angry muttering in the hall. Valerie makes it to the front window in time to see a car speed off into the night. Upstairs, a woman wails. Her voice rises then shudders into unremitting sobs, the very sound of heartbreak. It goes on for half an hour. Standing at the window, Valerie doesn't know if she should try to walk upstairs and knock, or call police, or just mind her business. She has no right to get involved, isn't sure if it's her place. But Nan is her friend, or at least someone close who is having a hard time. She dials upstairs.

The phone rings faintly through the ceiling, and the crying stops. Valerie thinks about her own stunned silence during her marriage, when the outside world interrupted her misery. She never could find the words to answer.

She lets the phone ring a few more times, then hangs up. Upstairs, the crying continues. She calls again, but no one answers. She waits by the phone.

The next morning, Nan calls with some excuse that James's number came up on the caller ID. Her voice sounds perfectly normal, pleasant even. It is a remarkable recovery.

"Are you sure? I thought I heard something fall up there," Valerie says. "If there's anything I can do . . ."

"Gosh, that's nice," Nan says. "But we're just fine. The cats have been tearing up a storm."

That's it. No mention of crying, fighting. The upstairs is quiet for several days but she never catches sight of Nan. Valerie worries that Nan is hiding bruises. The one time Valerie's husband slapped her, before she moved out, she called in sick for a week.

Then it starts again—crashing furniture, slamming doors. To her surprise, when she looks out the front window this time, she sees Nan getting in her car. James's phone rings.

"Hello, yes?" Valerie asks, thinking Nan might be calling from a cell phone. But it is Nan's home number on the caller ID. If Nan just left, who is calling?

"Hello?" she asks again.

There is no response.

"Can I help you?" Valerie asks, trying to picture the person upstairs, dialing down. Is this the abuser, reaching out to her? Trying to scare her off? Trying to tell his side of the story? Nothing makes any sense, and frankly, she's beginning to get spooked.

"I don't feel it's right to talk to you. Nan is my friend. Please don't call back." Valerie hangs up.

But what unnerves her, later, after she has checked all her doors, is the specific sound behind the silence. It wasn't threat. It was darker and more familiar: a drawing of breath, the gathering of effort. The sound was like the endless pause before her mother pushed out words. What she heard, she is almost certain, was someone's simple wish to speak.

Though she'll never give them any credit, it's the cats who solve the mystery. It isn't James, who calls one night while she is finishing off his pinot. It isn't her father, who only cares about her settlement from the accident, and it surely isn't Nan herself, since

Valerie is avoiding her. Things upstairs seem too dangerous, too overwhelming, for her to get involved. What happens is that Valerie gets mushy about the cats, despite their faults, because they care enough to sleep by her and fetch her little wads of paper. She reports this to James, who in a heartbeat, diminishes all she has accomplished.

"I though that would happen, and I'm glad," he says. "But as a rule, cats will do anything if you feed them. With cats, food is love."

But Valerie knows what they have is real. Paris amuses her by chasing corks, and Hector purrs in her arms, and they all have a wonderful time on the balcony, where Valerie sits and drinks. As the day drifts warmly into evening and fireflies start to blink, the hours blur into a pattern—meowing, opening the door, closing it, meowing, opening, closing, meowing—and in this way, Valerie startles awake one morning in an otherwise empty apartment. The cats are missing. Hector is on the balcony, thank God, cold and grumpy. But Paris is really gone, loose in the city, and who knows for how long. The balcony is an easy jump to the sidewalk, the busy streets. And so faster than she's moved in months, Valerie is dressed and out the door.

She walks through the small front courtyard, rattling the bag of treats—the sound, James says, of love. A noise—is it a cat meowing?—makes her turn and face the building. And then, a cat meows! Except the cat is really one of her neighbor's cats, perched in Nan's windowsill. Valerie's belly sinks. She starts to look away when she hears another sound, a human noise, the clearing of a throat. Standing behind Nan's cat is a shriveled, ancient woman, hunched and gray-haired. She is watching Valerie.

The front hedge rustles and Paris bolts out. Valerie grabs him and scratches his head, wondering if she has seen an apparition. But the woman in Nan's window is still standing there. The old woman raises her hand, a tiny wave. Then Nan appears behind the woman, who slowly turns away. Nan pulls the blind.

Walking inside, Valerie resolves to stay sober for at least today. She resolves to sit perfectly still and pet the cats and let everything return to normal.

Except it doesn't. Who was in the window? Was that Nan's mother? No one should talk to her mother like that, Valerie thinks. But then again, maybe it's the old woman yelling. Maybe she has dementia; maybe she screams all day at unseen things and topples furniture. Or maybe the situation is a combination of things. Maybe Nan takes care of her ailing mother and works hard and goes to school, and all of this together makes them both sharp, at odds. After all, just because the woman is old doesn't mean that she is nice. Yes, like her accident, maybe there are no good guys and bad guys, just shades of error and intention. A pair of forces, weak and strong, crashing, at a point.

If only she were equipped with Cass's sense of hearing. If only she could sort through everyday sounds, sift care and love from menace. But she can't even climb the stairs or control two skinny cats, or keep herself from pilfering her own dear brother's expensive wine. And so she sits alone beneath something strange and dark and weighty, poised above her head. She has nothing to offer anyone, not even so much as a prayer.

James returns. He's exhausted and leathery and stinks like a kayak, but he is home, and she shows him how well she can walk, then holds him close. The cats sniff him but weave through her legs, not his, and this makes Valerie happy. Still, she can't wait to leave. Of course, there is much she won't tell him: the missing cats, the missing wine, the fighting from above, the long days and nights without sleep.

"Did you make any friends," he asks, laughing, and about this, she is honest. "No, not one. There's no one here I want to know."

She is ready for the door to close behind her, for the wind to blow her hair. James wonders if his car will start, and he tells her to wait in front.

In the courtyard, Nan and a neighbor are edging the walkways with marigolds. They take each plant from a plastic tray and pat it into the ground. Tucked in the shade, sitting on a stool, is the old woman from the window. She wears a cardigan and large straw hat. She smiles at Valerie and raises her hand, that same odd gesture, not quite a wave.

Nan sits back on her knees. "Hi, Valerie. Are you leaving so soon? It seems like you just got here. You never met my mother, Ellen." Her voice becomes slow and deliberate as she touches her mother's shoulder. "Mom, this is the sister of the man who lives below us. She took care of his apartment."

The old woman moves her lips but it's some time before any words come out. "Valerie. You found. Your cat?"

Valerie nods, glad James is gone, glad he is readying the car. She wants to be moving on.

But the woman keeps talking, or trying to talk. "I saw. Your cat run. Into the bushes," she says. "He sure was. Glad. To see you."

"Boy, was he," Valerie answers brightly.

James pulls to the curb and she starts towards him. There, she thinks, looking back at them, Nan and her mother, planting flowers. Everything is fine with these people. Whatever their troubles, they have their peace. There is nothing she need do.

As she walks by the old woman, Valerie kicks over the tray of marigolds. She stoops and gathers the flowers, and for the first time, she notices the absence of pain. A faint twinge remains where grillwork hit her, but that is all. She wants to tell James, tell everyone. *I was hurt but I think I've recovered*, she could shout. It's how she might tell her mother, since no one has told her mother about the accident—that is, not yet. But Valerie is bursting with news and courage, maybe enough to make a visit. As Ellen reaches to gather the flowers, Valerie has the wild urge to hold that faltering hand.

That's when she sees them. A cluster of bruises, like a bracelet, around the old woman's wrist. The kind of bruises an old lady might get from falling, from poor balance, from lots of ordinary accidents, from throwing an arm out to catch herself before hitting the ground. You would expect that a daughter, a nurse, would pound across the floor to save her. Valerie is thinking this as she walks to the car, thinking such small bruises, five of them in a circle. Young and purple, in a familiar pattern. Could it be a face? She looks back at the woman as they pull away. She thinks how the woman pressed the window glass, raising her hand, almost waving, but how the gesture seemed more like showing, like holding a dark thought to the light. See, she was saying, five bruises, and look, here's five more, on my arm, on my neck, under my sweater. Wait, don't you see them, here are five bruises, fading like hope, round and tender as petals. Look now, come closer, bruises, they're everywhere—the largest no bigger than your thumb.

tom and georgia come over to swim

The night is too humid and still for the fan, but Pauline needs sound, the hum of blades slicing air. She twists the knob on the GE stand-up to "high," then spins around to cool the backs of her knees. Strips of red and pink plastic fly from the fan, circling and flickering over her skin like minnows. Last Saturday, Pauline's daughter Ellie tied streamers to the fan after watching the air-conditioning display at Sears. Ellie had liked the way the display's silver-blue streamers glinted and danced in cool air. Pauline likes the noise of the streamers as they tangle together, crackling over the hum like her daughter's laughter.

She twirls again, as if her motion will help stir the air, but her knees remain sticky, the breeze damp and mechanical. She walks to the kitchen and opens the freezer, leaning deep into iced shelves of boxed waffles and paper-wrapped T-bones. Lingering in the chill, she takes out an ice tray; she'll have a quick Beam and Coke before Tom and Georgia arrive. She'll mix it light, pouring almost all Coke: a little something sweet and cool on her throat, but with enough edge and weight to steel her insides.

Pauline was surprised to see Tom and Georgia at the 5-Star today, out and about, even shopping, like any other day. Since their daughter Carrie's funeral a few weeks ago, it seems like their front door hasn't opened, though cars line the curb all the way to Pauline's mailbox. Every time she drives by, Pauline is struck by how everything outside—the volleyball net and plump rhododendrons—looks exactly the same. But when she wheeled her cart into produce this morning, there they stood, Georgia touching the rough husks of cantaloupes, Tom staring at the grapes in the cart. Pauline chattered stupidly about the clumsy new paperboy, the slow mail this week, anything just to fill the silence between them. Pauline noticed their cart was absent of its usual fruit pops and cereal. Her own cart seemed too full of such things, garish with cartoon colors.

At the 5-Star, Pauline talked too eagerly for too long a time, but she at least had the sense to invite Tom and Georgia to swim. It was, she felt, her only comfort to offer. The last few days of July have been the hottest in years, the air stifling, almost like trying to breathe water. Pauline's husband Danny drooped through the doorway this evening, his shirt clinging, the very soul sweated out of him from working all day at their landscaping business. The pool, she hopes, will bring sweet relief to them all.

She cracks ice into a glass, each cube dropping and ringing through the kitchen and hall. Lately, Pauline has noticed that silence seems amplified, that background noises are strangely essential and soothing. Especially when she is alone, like tonight: Danny has run to the Quik-Mart for beer, and Ellie is upstairs asleep, exhausted from another full day of play. This summer has brought Ellie's friends like cicadas, their voices from the back-yard loud and cheerful and constant. They splash in the pool, scream "Marco! Polo!" and shriek as suits are yanked and hand-stands collapse. Pauline usually watches over the pages of a *People*, keeping a close eye on Ellie, watching as Ellie plays water ballet. She thinks there is nothing so graceful as when her daughter kicks high to the clouds, her legs proud and slender as a swan's neck, curling in at the toes. Her legs hover, then slowly disappear into underwater darkness like the rest of her, without even a ripple. Ellie has practiced this move since she was just seven, and now at eight, has added a downward half-spiral. Still, Pauline counts every second until the water breaks, until the sub-merged shadow bursts into form and becomes her daughter again.

Pauline stands by Ellie's bed, her drink clinking softly; she holds the glass tighter to muffle the sound. Her daughter is sweating through dreams but is safe and intact, kicking off covers and sheets as she sleeps. She slides her cooled fingers across Ellie's bangs, over her bright, sunburned cheeks. Ellie folds her-self in and away from the touch.

The garage door opens and voices echo through the down-stairs: Danny laughing, offering a cold beer to Tom; Georgia declining, she brought one from home. Danny calls, "Pauline! Where are you, woman?" She takes four towels from the closet and walks down.

Tom and Georgia stand at the kitchen table, holding Bud-weiser cans sleeved in red plastic coolers. Danny talks about the heat as he loads a case of beer into the refrigerator. He removes the potato salad, containers of Kool-Aid, ketchup and pickles, steadily replacing each with more cans. Walking past him, Pauline places her drink by the sink, then takes the potato salad from the counter to put it back on a shelf.

"It's a wonder we don't all die of food poisoning around here," she says to Georgia, then stops herself, horrified. They've been in her kitchen one minute and already Pauline has mentioned death. She stares at the Kool-Aid.

But Georgia rolls her eyes. She pulls a chair from the table and sits beside Tom. "Really, Danny," she says, chiding. "Why is it you men don't have any sense?"

Tom nods to Danny, raising his can in the air. "Look, he's got his priorities straight: beer first. *That's* sense for you. Right, Danny?" His laugh is quiet, all breath without sound.

"You tell them, Tom," Danny says. "These wives of ours think they know it all." He sits at the table.

Pauline stands at the counter, uncertain, in need of a task. "How about some food? I think I have clam dip somewhere in here."

"That's okay, Pauline," Georgia says. "Don't trouble yourself. We've eaten already."

Tom nods. "People have brought us so many dishes and casseroles. We had Eleanor Compton's chicken-something tonight. It had those little cornflake pieces on the top."

"I think they were onion rings, Tom," Georgia says. "It's just been so hard to cook." She pulls her curly brown hair behind each ear and traces the top of her can. Her fingernail polish is chipped, picked off like Ellie's sparkle polish. It's not like Georgia. She has always looked cute and little and lively, wearing earrings even with sweat pants, nail color to match.

"Everyone's cooking has been a big help. Thanks again, Pauline, for your lasagna. We've frozen it," Tom says.

Then everyone is quiet. Too quiet. For too long a time. Danny drums his hands on the edge of the table. He purses his lips like he's going to whistle, and Pauline wills him to speak, to talk of their new grill or deck chairs, anything to lift the mood closing in. The air thickens. The overhead light burns her skin. Her husband taps the table again and again.

Pauline tries to come up with something to talk about. If this were any other night, she and Georgia would kvetch and gossip about their daughters. Last time they got together, Georgia was worried about Carrie's first boyfriend, who Tom called The Groper, and Carrie's fascination with her budding cleavage. "The kids these days. Did we ever wear anything so revealing?" Georgia asked. Pauline agreed—she had already caught Ellie hip-swiveling and butt-wiggling in front of the T.V. like her favorite pop stars. They reminisced about the shoulder pads and parachute pants and surfer shirts of their own teenage fashion—terrible as it was, at least it covered you. Then they laughed about what old ladies they'd become. All evening, as Pauline refilled their drinks, she and Georgia would clink glasses and say things like "In my day, we wore hemlines down to our ankles!" and "Whatever happened to those practical bloomers?" When Tom and Georgia came over to swim, evenings could turn silly like that, spinning Pauline far away from the tensions of managing their business—the sloth and graft of the seasonal crews, the temperament of flowers.

Now they all sit at the table, silent and sweating. It occurs to her to get the fan. She carries it into the kitchen, placing it in the windowsill by the table. When she turns the switch, the fan churns the air into wind, and the streamers twist and snap at their ears. Tom's longish hair whips across Georgia's face. Pauline's tank top flutters like the moths at the screens.

"How refreshing," Danny yells above the noise.

"Sorry, sorry," Pauline yells, cutting the switch down to low. She wants to laugh, but isn't sure if that's something they can do now. Georgia pulls a long, blond hair from her lips. Tom looks at Georgia, then Pauline, then Danny.

"You guys never could entertain worth a damn," Tom says. His whisper laugh rises, and Pauline is relieved.

Georgia looks at Pauline and smiles. "So, how about that swim?" she asks. Lifting the stack of beach towels from the counter, she walks out to the deck, and the men follow.

Pauline hesitates by the counter. Georgia's smile had been toothy and perfectly shaped, but her eyes seemed hollow, carved of all substance. Suddenly, she wants to hold Georgia's hands. At the memorial service, Georgia had squeezed her hand so hard that Pauline thought her own fingers would splinter. Now she wonders if those fingers would still curl into hers, could manage even that most basic reflex, or if they would just slip away.

She adds bourbon to her drink and walks out to the deck. "I was just showing Tom the new grill," Danny says as she hands him a new beer.

Georgia sits in a chair and removes her shirt. Sitting beside her, Pauline can't help but stare at her pale neck and shoulders. The deck lights cast Georgia's body as a landscape of bones and shadows, like the sockets of trees in a newly stripped yard.

". . . And these chairs, and those lights by the pool," Danny tells Tom. "Pauline, how much did those lights cost? Remember, at Sears?" He points to each, talking on, motioning assembly and wiring.

Pauline can't recall prices or even selecting the lights and the chairs. She can think only of the air conditioning display, of Ellie's face as she watched, mesmerized, crunching on her favorite Sears candy: small chocolates covered in tiny, white beads.

"Ellie made us look everywhere for bike streamers to put on the fan," she says to Georgia. "She saw the display, you know that display that they have? Well, you've seen our fan." She realizes too late that she's talked of her daughter.

Georgia nods, looking out at the pool. "Carrie used to stare at that like she was watching T.V. She'd also climb all over the rounders and racks, until Tom called her 'monkey girl,' and made her so mad she stopped." She sips her beer. Pauline sips her drink.

"Hey, are we just going to look at that pool?" Danny asks. He nudges Pauline. "Come on, ladies, less talking, more stripping. Look at Georgia, she's ready. She's waiting on you."

He clamps his hand onto Georgia's shoulder. His knuckles, always dirty no matter how hard he scrubs, look alarmingly clumsy and huge. Pauline tries to remember a time when she wasn't apologizing for her husband in some way, ducking her head in a crowd when he whoops and hollers, sharing a what-I-put-up-with smile with other wives at barbecues. Lately, it's only when he is with their daughter—when he helps Ellie swing a bat or hides Easter eggs—that she glimpses the man she thought she married. When he becomes someone more tender, more complicated: more like herself.

He pulls off his T-shirt and pitches it at Pauline. She catches it and folds it. "You with me, Tom?" he asks, dipping a toe in the pool.

"With you, Dan, my man," Tom calls, pulling off his own shirt. His stomach sags furry and soft over his trunks, but he doesn't, for once, joke that the baby is kicking.

They walk past the slide to the deep end and jump. Pauline wipes the splash from her arm. "We'd better get in ourselves, before they club and drag us," she says to Georgia, pulling off her tank top and shorts, twisting her hair in a bun.

Georgia stands and shakes her khaki shorts from her hips, then removes her turquoise earrings. "Do you think these will be okay over here?" she asks, placing them on the table along with her shorts.

The earrings look vulnerable to splashes and bumps. "I could put them inside," Pauline offers.

Georgia agrees and follows her in the house. "Carrie bought these for me in Arizona," she says.

"That's right, you guys have New York coming up." It is out of Pauline's mouth before she can stop it. Tom and Georgia and

Carrie took trips every August, to wonderful places Danny and Pauline can't afford: Disneyworld, Vancouver, Mackinac Island. They would bring pictures over and everyone would sit by the pool, squinting at snapshots until sunset turned to candlelight and the girls got antsy. Without thinking, Pauline has mentioned the next trip they'd planned. Carrie had been hoping to see celebrities and, Georgia confided, to be discovered. They were supposed to go shopping on 5th Avenue right away and no one was allowed to wear fanny packs or cameras, or else they'd stick out like dopey tourists. They had snagged impossible-to-get tickets to a Broadway show. Tom had sent for a subway map. He was learning the routes.

"Georgia, I'm sorry. Danny's right, I talk too much, " Pauline says.

Georgia's eyes are bright and moist. Her cheeks are flushed. "Do you have a tissue?"

"Sure. Hang on." Pauline runs to the bathroom and grabs the box. Maybe this is what their evenings will come to, at least for awhile, until things get back to normal: Pauline tripping and spilling wherever she steps, then rushing like mad to tidy up. In the meantime, she is sure there will be things to talk about. Danny's plans to lay the back walkway with paverbrick, for example. Whether or not to incorporate their business. Where to find good deals on hoses and floor cleaners. Conversations usually left to the men.

She walks out of the bathroom and nearly tramples her daughter, who is standing there, hair tangled, eyes vacant. Sleepwalking. It started the night after Carrie's funeral. Pauline was lying in bed, listening to Danny's heavy, wet breathing, when in the bedroom window she saw Ellie's reflection gliding down the hall. It scared the daylights out of her. She called a psychologist friend who told her Ellie was processing the trauma and her reaction was normal; just clear a path and coax her to bed. Now, no matter how exhausted she is, she waits for her daughter to rise and wander, trying to guide her up steps, around corners, without letting her wake.

"Come on now, Ellie," Pauline says. "Let's get you back upstairs."

"It's in the garage," Ellie mumbles.

"Okay. You can get it tomorrow," Pauline says, steering her through the living room. Suddenly, Georgia is standing right in front of them.

"Sleepwalking," Pauline whispers. She hands Georgia the tissue box.

Georgia nods. She stares at Ellie for a moment, then smiles— a tight, almost embarrassed smile—and turns back towards the kitchen.

Pauline guides Ellie up the stairs. Working her daughter into bed, Pauline's throat closes as she thinks of the look on Georgia's face. After shock, before she smiled and turned away, there had been something else, something worse: a small, almost imperceptible, elation. The astonished delight of misrecognition. A blonde girl in a hallway when such things seemed impossible.

Pauline strokes Ellie's back, hoping her daughter will take root. She looks around the room. On the floor, Ellie's swimsuit lies twisted; her kicked-off shorts still hold her shape. Pauline is struck with a feeling of overabundance and walks downstairs to shake it off.

Pouring a fresh drink, she looks out the window and sees Georgia at the water's edge. Pauline gathers a new round of beers and walks out. Pauline makes her way into the pool. She wades down the concrete steps until water laps at her shoulders. Georgia sits on a step and leans back on her elbows, facing the men in the deep end, who flip and dive to the bottom. After splashing each other, Danny and Tom swim over. They sit on the steps.

"Feels wonderful, huh?" Danny asks. Tom and Georgia nod, floating their arms on the surface. The lights of the pool make their skin seem colorless, almost transparent. Pauline feels her suntan like weight.

Tom cups water and drips it like rain from his fingers. Georgia looks towards the sky, which is scattered with stars. Pauline looks up. If she squints, Pauline can make out the faint clouds of the Milky Way. She searches the horizon for the crooked handle of the Big Dipper, then for the planet she always mistakes for the North Star. She remembers Danny teaching Ellie how to locate Orion: just look for three bright stars together, and you've found his belt.

"Does anyone need another beer?" Danny asks.

No one is quick to respond. Georgia rests her head on the ledge, her eyes on the stars. Tom sieves the water through his hands. Danny and Pauline look at each other. Danny raises his eyebrows in the way they've developed to send messages around Ellie, but the night is so shadowy, Pauline can't comprehend. They have been doing that a lot lately, missing signals, forgetting simple things. At the greenhouse they've had screaming fights over yellowing vinca vines, drowned ornamentals, trays of blue-moon lobelia left to crisp in the sun. Afterwards, a hard silence settles between them. Around Ellie, for her sake, they soften and tease. In the evenings, even though she's too old for it now, she lays her head in Pauline's lap and makes Danny play this-little-piggy with her toes. Their daughter stretches between them, a thin, bright bridge with skinned knees, keeping them comfortably linked, together and apart.

Now, Tom says, "I'm sorry you guys. Today was hard for us. It was real hard for Georgia." He looks at some far place behind Pauline. "The coroner's report came. In the mail. You know, right there with the catalogs."

It is unbelievable, Pauline thinks. Who would send a thing like that in the mail?

"It said that Carrie had brain injuries," Tom says. "'Massive internal contusions, cranial fractures.' All documented, labeled and signed. It broke us. Ridiculous, isn't it? I mean, of all things to get upset about these days. A stupid piece of paper."

Pauline wants to change the subject. But how? Where are the things they used to talk about? There must be some way to talk about one of those things again. Window boxes, school shopping, the block party, room additions. Wasn't there anything normal, anything untouched?

Danny reaches over and pats Tom on the back. "I'm sorry," he says.

"Thanks, Danny. I mean that. This is nice of you guys. Really. You've been a big help to us. Everyone has. I guess some folks put a little marker there, at the intersection. A wreath."

She focuses on the water, her shapeless body beneath, but Pauline can't distract herself from the scene: the road, the blinding sunlight of evening, the crumpled frame of Carrie's new mountain bike. The intersection, bordered by a pumpkin patch on one side; the pumpkins still small, tucked close to the vine.

"When it gets real bad, like today, we visit her. We visit the grave," Tom continues.

But Pauline wants him to stop. She has already seen it in her head a thousand times: the charcoal gray marble, the etched name, the dates that are too close together to be real, to be right. The sky was cloudless and dazzling on the day of the funeral; a perfect day for the pool, she had thought, dressing Ellie. Surely, Georgia wants Tom to stop talking about it, too, but Georgia's eyes haven't moved from the sky, from the stars.

"Visit the grave," Danny says, puzzled. "Does that help? I would think it would just make you sadder."

"No, it actually helps us," Tom says. "We always come away feeling better than when we came. Like we've connected with her in a way, I guess."

Danny nods. "Hey, if you want anything special there, you know, like a small tree or flowers, we've got you covered."

"Hmm," Tom says. "That's an idea. We'll have to talk it over." He's quiet for a minute. He looks at Pauline. "The other day we saw Jack Wilson, he was visiting Jason. He's two rows over from Carrie. You remember Jason, don't you?"

Pauline nods. Jason was a strapping red-haired boy who delivered the morning paper. But she doesn't want to think about Jason, swept away in a drainpipe, while everyone on the block waited for news. She doesn't want to remember how she held Ellie and Carrie, both so little then, as the police car drove up the street and stopped in Jack's driveway. She doesn't want to see the girls peeking through the living room curtains, giggling, as Jason rolled his papers. There was no point in remembering any of it. She doesn't want to think about Carrie splashing in the pool, bursting through waves, stretching her long, tanned legs to the sky, spitting water through braces at Ellie, laughing. She doesn't want to see Carrie teaching Ellie handsprings, keeping Ellie from falling, turning her, gently, head over heels. But she doesn't know how to see anything else. She looks at Georgia. Georgia hasn't moved from the step, hasn't even rippled the water. Her eyes remain on the stars.

Georgia whispers, "I still have to do laundry."

And Pauline understands. She can see Carrie's jumpers, her pink jeans, her tank tops, her overalls, piled in baskets, waiting to be washed, dried and worn. Carrie's shoes, wet from walking through the meadow with her boyfriend, still dry on the welcome mat in back of their house. Tucked in the back of a drawer where her mother isn't supposed to look, Carrie's old sweatshirts hide daisy-print push-up bras. Sleek black pants and silky blouses hang in her closet, ready to shine on the streets of New York. Her yellow bikini hangs in the bathroom, on the towel rack; Ellie always stood on her tiptoes to help tie the straps. Nearby is Pauline's beach towel, lent weeks ago. That is only the laundry.

Pauline slides through the water to sit next to Georgia. She reaches and finds Georgia's hand, and she lifts it, cradling it into her own. Georgia's fingers curl slowly. Following Georgia's eyes to the horizon, Pauline is sure that they're both searching for Orion, for three stars strung together on the black summer sky.

simple as that

If she is to grieve, Lila reasons, she will do so Hollywood-style, with exaggerated gestures, crescendoing sobs, flowing gowns that sweep her ankles. After searching her closet for diva-wear, she wraps herself in a pink bathrobe the shade and texture of marshmallow candy. The robe is spectacular—the perfect pitch of melodrama. It is a Christmas present from her mother, who has long tried to kindle Lila's theatricality. Last week, her mother sent a box of beaded dragonfly hair-clips that flutter from silver springs. One jiggles over Lila's bangs. Inside the robe, Lila is tiny and rigid. She feels like she's in drag.

Still, she wants to wrap her sorrow in a turban, bejewel it fabulously, ride it to the hilt. *Hilt* is a word she never uses; the robe is making Lila think in a new vocabulary, in words like *horror!* and *splendid!*, in exclamation points, in vibrato. Wearing the robe makes her want to taffy-pull despair until it snaps and disappears.

Wearing the robe, she believes it's possible for sorrow to be whipped into frothy peaks—to be made confectionery—and so dissolve, melt away like sugar in rain. It seems possible that in this way, her husband's absence could shrink to granules, something easily evaporated. Something that would leave and actually stay gone, and not return for forgotten books or visits with the dog.

But he does not want to stay gone, her husband tells her at every chance he gets. He does not want the marriage to be over. He calls from work every day and leaves rumbly, rambling messages. He e-mails her with haikus for their dog, with the requisite lines about sniffing, peeing, birding. He attempts good cheer on a limited budget. In their separation, he constantly surprises her with clichés, and this, along with everything, is very disappointing. Lila had expected more from him, something swashbuckling in reconciliation. But then, she had also expected a more innovative break-up. In fact, what enrages her lately is that the break-up has made her a cliché—a jilted wife, a spurned spouse, a Dear Abby archetype. *Couldn't you be more original?* she had screamed at him from her car phone on the day she fled, the Day of Discovery. She was driving distant country roads looking for motels, sleet spitting at her windshield, when he called her car to plead forgiveness. He rationalized: *It didn't mean anything, it happened once and now it's totally over.* He was trying to negotiate Lila's surrender, trying to talk her in. But Lila held herself hostage and drove to a Motel 6. Huddled in her car in the parking lot, she told him to move out; her three-year marriage was ending, like a junior high break-up, in a histrionic phone call. When all was said and done, she still couldn't believe the sheer triteness of it all: a strange credit card receipt, an other woman, a *blonde,* for heaven's sake. *I thought you writers were supposed to be more creative!* she had yelled into the car phone, her words floating through an open channel, carried over public airwaves so that somewhere, she was certain, perverts and sixth graders gleefully collected the cells of her distress.

But tonight, the pink cloud of the robe envelops her and softens edges, smears Vaseline on the lens of memory, and pulling the collar tight, Lila tries to locate a clean glass in the wreckage of their—now her—kitchen counter. Lately, she has been overwhelmed by the simple mechanics of order and nutrition. Looking around, it seems unreal that the kitchen was once a bustling, aromatic place, where she and her husband cracked peppercorns and sautéed shrimp in spontaneous sauces. That kitchen is a foreign country where they made weekend soups from scratch. And oh! the bounty once housed here—leeks, turmeric, andouille sausage. But now, crystallized ginger looks to her like mutant raisins or mummified kidneys. Feeding has been reduced to binary steps: toasting, buttering. Boiling, pouring. Microwaving, rotating. Her major food group consists of hydrogenated oils baked into various shapes—some cream-filled, some with corners. Lila worries about folic acid. "I've been eating nothing but cheese and crackers for dinner for two weeks," she has told her mother. "At least you're getting calcium," her mother encourages. "Calcium and grains."

It occurs to her that being alone could be more fun if she had a tall, bright cup to sip from. Healing could be as simple as that. Beneath a Poptart wrapper, she finds a notepad and writes a Thing To Do: *Stop Moping Around! Buy Cute Tumblers!* She has never imagined writing such a Thing. Perhaps the pink robe is making her write this. Perhaps the dragonfly hair-clip is channeling messages from her mother. It is, after all, a night charged with psychic potential—thunderheads crackle the evening sky.

This spring has been turbulent, with hard snowfalls and explosive blossoms, pre-dawn thunderstorms that bring Lila's dog bounding onto her husband's side of the bed. Of course, she wishes that the weather, too, could be more original—could offer more than song titles or film noir—especially when she's suffering. But beyond their capacity for cruel metaphor, the storms are terrifying, and she has taken to moving her Chagall wedding print from the wall to the pantry every night. For a week, the storms have hit around four in the morning, whipping small trees onto the Interstate and clogging the morning rush hour. Downtown, people yawn on the streets, move flaccidly, thudding into each other with mumbled apology. In the food court where she lunches, strangers linger on benches to recount near-disasters: the sirens that sent them scurrying to basements, the trees uprooted, the shingles or sandbox toys swept into sky. Babies loll, invertebrate, in their strollers. Children are quick to whine. Lila watches and listens but eats alone, somehow soothed by murmured weariness. She is not in the mood for conversation; these days, even consonants seem like effort. Before the storms, she occasionally ate with Cindy, the other human resource secretary in her department-store office, but Cindy is a Pentecostal, and though Lila isn't sure about their policies, the weather has rooted Cindy to her desk, where she reads the Bible instead of grabbing a cheesesteak.

The T.V. weathermen have become over-earnest, and now, like every other evening, most of the news is devoted to Doppler projections, battening tips, the sturdiest interior locations. Some of the channels quiz the audience on hail formation; some maps take viewers on rollicking rides through developing systems. Lila imagines it must be comforting to map and scale upheaval. On the screen behind one weathercaster, wind and rainfall intensities spiral in rainbow bands, swirling around the patchy Metro area like a tie-dye shirt design. It is horrifying and beautiful.

It is possible, she realizes, that she could die in a storm, alone, on the couch, in this robe, a dragonfly clip sproinging from her severed head. Dead at thirty in a pink confection, a beaded insect in her hair. She wells at the thought—not because in the thought, she is dead, but because it reminds her of a game she and her husband used to play, a game borne of their own bad habits: *What Would the Coroner Think?* As a child, Lila had been fascinated by the T.V. show *Quincy,* the way Jack Klugman linked a drowned teenager to bad weed, or traced killer spores to a stadium water fountain. For awhile, during puberty, she made it a practice to pack clues to her death somewhere on her body: if the Skittles she was eating looked old and funny, she left three in the pack, tucked in her pocket for later forensic testing. Even then, she was the kind of person who tried to make things easier for others.

With her husband, though, the game had grown sillier, especially when they left the apartment untended—when the laundry heaped and they wore desperate, ratty things, when all of their light bulbs burned out and they squinted like moles to find each other. Still, Lila knows there are worse ways to be found. She recalls the story her husband told of a body discovered in a caretaker's apartment above a fitness club—a body wrapped entirely in athletic tape, with red high heels poking out. Nobody was aware of the caretaker's murderous tendencies, but suspiciously, he was missing, too. When the police untaped the body, of course, they found the missing man dead inside, an amazing case of auto-erotic asphyxiation. It was no wonder the red high heels were size thirteen and very, very wide. For crowds, her husband usually ended the story with *I just hope I die with a smile on my face!* Alone, with her, when he wanted to appear soulful, he finished with a line from his favorite poem: *There is no telling what we'll do in our fierce drive to come together.* Fierce drive. No telling. She considers this as she flips through T.V. weathermen. Should she have noticed his fondness for this poem? Was her husband tagging his own dying fidelity, tucking clues into the pockets of something he would later kill?

That's the thing about the traumatized, she knows from listening to herself, to her own wronged friends—they are so *boring,* so undyingly morbid. Terminal with their own darkness, the woe-ful could smother every light conversation, kill off all diversion. But the pink candy robe should protect her from solemnity. She thinks now she should wear the robe to bed. Some mornings, she wakes with mysterious aches. Sometimes she calls in sick. It has been too easy lately to lie in bed until noon, leaden with gravity; when she finally rises, she expects her body will have grooved the mattress like a snow angel. Lila is new to negativity. She is sur-prised by angry voices in her head, hateful characters who never existed before, not even when her husband waggled his finger at her numerous domestic failures. But being stunned—really stunned—has unleashed Lila's cattiness, which has taken form in a campy voice that surfaces randomly to mock. A large woman in a bright green dress might walk up to her desk in search of a job, and handing her an application, Lila thinks *Mm-Mmm! You can't wear that honey, that's why God made the watermelon.* Or when Bill, the ancient store detective, strides heroically by, the campy voice clucks *If brains were dynamite, that man couldn't blow his nose.* Lila resents her husband for creating this voice inside her head. She doesn't want to think like this. She is such a nice person, inside and out—so full of integrity she never reveals people's salaries, never gossips about who's taking lithium or neglecting child sup-port. When she senses people may be talking about her, even nicely, she covers her ears and walks away. She really, really does.

At seven-thirty, her husband calls, which is odd because his apartment does not have a phone. However, he has taken up jog-ging to gas stations, and as he leaves a message, Lila hears city noises in the background. The station bell dings as he says he loves her; a siren rises as he says he misses her. He bids her a good night's sleep to the enormous whoosh of a bus. He says he will be over tomorrow to walk the dog, the sad custody arrangement they've hammered while she thinks things over—while he goes, and she goes, and they all go to therapy. Therapy has become something to conjugate, and Lila knows conjugation well. Despite the fact that she's now a secretary, she has a Master's in English Education, and her teacher's training volunteers itself at inappropriate times. Like now: Lila is constantly struck by the grammar of separation, the renaming, the claiming, the circuitry of language. Pronouns have acquired a newfound importance. Moving out, her husband resented the couch Lila called "*my* couch," even though it was. She loathes his account of the affair "*We* decided had to stop," and can't help wondering when, exactly, *he* joined someone else's *we*. She reprimands his passive constructions: "No, you can't say 'There was kissing.' Where's the Subject? Your *we* is the Subject." Still, Lila is weary of being the Object of impossible, bullying active verbs. So what if she can diagram loss? Appositives, despite their optimism, never successfully restructure the rubble. The meaning always remains the same. No matter how he tells it, no matter how she grades, her husband's story can never pass.

On the advice of her therapist, she decides to take a relaxing herbal bath. The robe makes her pour seven capfuls of bubbles beneath the faucet, and to honor the hair clip, she roots through facial cremes until she finds one that hasn't calcified. Upon noticing her absent wedding ring, Lila's boss recommended Pastoral therapy, which Lila—trained to cull meaning from context— assumed would take place in the country, or with a preacher, or with a country preacher. Her boss gave Lila the name of a personal friend, and so Lila had to make an appointment, and so today she left work early to drive angrily through traffic. The therapist's office was located above a store called Cabinet Masters. The therapist, Jaden, was fortyish, with long gray hair and light, serene eyes that Lila associated with Californians. She wore loose, maroon clothes and carved stone pendants. When she opened her office door, the smell of sage drifted out, and Lila was surprised to see a waterfall fountain and a pillowy bed surrounded by tall plants. This did indeed seem like the country, or perhaps a country all its own.

"I just want to honor you for coming here today," the therapist began.

Lila immediately felt awkward, and said, "It's an . . . honor . . . to be honored." She had never been to therapy before, and didn't want to do it wrong; what if she had a total breakdown right there, in the office, and had to be hauled away?

Next, Jaden, if that was her real name, spent ten minutes discussing her fee, which Lila, embarrassingly, had to negotiate. She joked that she was a payroll secretary who earned almost next to nothing. "I should work harder on my figure . . . s," she laughed, trying to make a good impression, trying to show the wit of someone trained to teach the puns of Shakespeare. Jaden smiled in a way that seemed to transcend the earthly and the material, but still wrote on Lila's patient form: "Further Sessions Subject to Full Fee." The rest of the session went downhill from there. No matter how tightly she closed her eyes, Lila couldn't imagine herself as a disc of spinning sunlight, big enough to beam all over the city, all over the world, when even watching T.V. weather maps made her slightly carsick. She couldn't cosmically rise and shine; even her breathing was too shallow to match Jaden's tranquil sighs. All she could think was if she were a wheel of sunlight, she'd burn her husband to a crisp like an ant trapped under glass.

And if she could be the sun, she wouldn't have paid eighty dollars for this handout on self-care advice: *Drink cocoa. Cry for thirty minutes. Hit a pillow. Give yourself a facial.* As the bath water foams, Lila checks off each of these, removes her *gay!* and *marvelous!* robe, and steps into the tub to *Soak troubled thoughts away.* Healing could be as simple as that. Lather, rinse, repeat.

Through the bathroom window, lightning flashes, and Lila tries to recall what the weathermen said about bathing in thunderstorms. She is not on a golf course, not under a tree, not talking on a cordless phone. Still, she is in water, surrounded by gleaming metal fixtures. She interrogates the bathtub: Does it matter if the tub is porcelain? Is porcelain considered a grounding material? What, exactly, is a grounding material? Is the tub she's sitting in even porcelain? She wonders if, sitting here, she could *complete the circuit,* a phrase she vaguely understands, but which is accompanied by a terrible image: a local electrician slumped over his own dryer, discovered by his wife, who couldn't even touch his still-thrumming body. *What would the coroner think?* The coroner reported the poor electrician had *completed the circuit*—and Lila doesn't know how not to. These are things her husband knows, things Lila hasn't had to study, like which screwdriver tightens the bathroom door hinge, which red wine gives her a headache.

For a moment, she considers the lightning, the nature of the word *shock*. Until now, she had thought it cliché when people said a discovery was *shocking*. She was a little cynical when Darcy in Cosmetics said she was *shocked* to learn that her sister was gay. And she thought old Security Bill exaggerated when he said his son's dishonorable discharge *hit him like a lightning bolt*. Such expressions were, she had once thought, hyperbole. But now the words seem remarkably apt. She still thrums with the burn of discovery. All the circuits in her body, her brain, seem to be rewired; all the ganglia clinging to her marriage have been swiftly cauterized. Like lightning victims who develop strange powers, Lila now sometimes sees the mall crowds with a new and special vision—a sensitivity to blight, a keen awareness of secret griefs that people hide in hollows. To Lila, these spaces shine like an aura. Yesterday, a glow alighted the man at the fountain who offered his daughter sips of Coke. Was he giving his daughter a "dad's night out," a break to his wife, who lounged at home leafing *Talbot's?* Or was this his weekly Visitation, like her husband's long Saturday walks with the dog? Watching the man and the girl, Lila wondered if it was always awkward between them. She wondered if he still felt shock that he no longer book-ended his daughter's days. No, *shock* and *lightning*, these were not hyperbole. Suddenly, she has the perfect title for her diva-memoir, the agonizing story of her first marriage and inspiring recovery: *It Was Never Hyperbole!* She resolves to write Chapter One tomorrow.

She also resolves to ignore the lightning that is flashing more rapidly outside her windowsill—a windowsill she can't help but notice is lined with metal objects. Fittingly, the instruments of her doom were once wedding gifts: a chrome canister for cotton puffs, an ivy-coiled towel rack. She traces a Rube-Goldberg-path from a lightning strike to the window ledge, to the canister to the towel rack to the faucet, down the stream of water pouring from the faucet, to her big toenail and the rest of her naked body. Could the dragonfly clip's metal spring serve as a lightning rod? *That* would certainly be one for the coroner. She is pleased that in some ways, she can still think generously.

But the coroner would have to wonder about the black fabric paint on her fingernails, stubborn under the washcloth, and for clues, he might have to ask her husband. In fact, she would like her husband to be interrogated, or at least made to feel guilty about the wickedness of the separation—its awful, spiteful timing. To make matters worse for Lila these days, Julia in Furs is getting married in May, and Lila is a bridesmaid. Julia's bachelorette party is next weekend, and for a party game, Lila has been charged with drawing and cutting out twenty life-sized penises from pink felt. "Of course, every penis should be felt," she had quipped to her dog as she cut and sketched. It seemed like a joke her husband would enjoy. An advertising copywriter, he understood the value of a pun: his biggest campaign had been a tennis promotion slugged "The Agony . . . and the Agassi." Humor drew them together, and sometimes it winks at them, even now. Her husband jokes about the pathetic state of his new apartment—the ironing board that hosts a Frisbee for an ashtray and various unidentifiable food stains. Healing could be as simple as that. Laugh and the world laughs with you.

If nothing else, she recalls with a sigh, he always laughed at her jokes, which, because of her special training, Lila thought to be exceptionally droll. In graduate school, she learned the anatomy of humor: burlesque, parody, low and high comedy, Juvenalian satire. She has been trained, for example, to know that the fact she now works as a secretary is not exactly *irony*; it would be more correct to say that it is *ironic* that she knows she is not living in irony. It is also correctly ironic that she trained to spend her whole life molding youth when she realized, suddenly before a class of seventh graders who kept giggling when she said "period," that she really hated kids. All of them, in all their forms—for Lila, there are no redeeming ages. Her husband, on the other hand, relates well to toddlers. It might also be *ironic,* she notes, that the storm outside is whipping into a frenzy—a frenzy in a series, a frenzy amply forecasted—and she can't imagine where on earth her husband has stored the flashlights.

Is it possible that he has taken all the flashlights? Is it possible that he isn't just weak and self-centered, but truly diabolical?

She pictures her husband sitting in his apartment, all their flashlights trained on his hands, fashioned dumbly into horses' heads. Although they've camped many times, her husband is still a hand-shadow amateur, relying on Lila's bats and lions to perk up his adventures. Because he is limited to horses and dogs, his plots are usually Westerns. As a clap of thunder rolls the sky, Lila reasons that if he forgot saline solution when he moved out, he likely left the flashlights. But he has no phone, so she can't ask him where they are, and despite herself, she hopes he hasn't ventured out in this weather. For now, she thinks it would be sad if he died at any hands but her own.

Still, this is not quite tenderness. Tenderness matters to her husband, who seeks a soft spot to plant himself again. He wants to improve and have her notice; he wants her not to harden. He plies her with take-out Indian food and poems on her sexier parts. It matters to him that Tuesday nights, they still watch detective shows together, even though in the lulls between programs, they fight and he begs and she sobs. He searches for a place where repentance can find purchase, a sidewalk crack where a seed might land and grow beneath the concrete. But Lila can only see the marriage for its craters, its pits. It may as well be moonscape. In fact, long before the separation, they'd poked sticks in rocky soil: they didn't embrace so much as pat and detach; they left the bathroom door open; they rolled their eyes and mocked each other in explosions over dry cleaning. She tried but could no longer ignore the way his teeth gnashed over forks. Then he started discussing children. She had assumed he wanted babies to justify why they never went out anymore.

The lights waver then hold, and the dog runs up to the tub. "It's okay, Beaker," she tells the dog, a regal German shepherd named for their favorite Muppet character. Now seems a good time to rise and dress and batten down. She stands quickly and reaches for a towel, when there's a terrible pop by the window ledge. Beaker whines. The lights disappear.

Lila stands naked, calf-deep in water, surrounded by silent blackness. The coroner would think *You took a bath in a thunderstorm? Didn't you watch the local forecast?* She feels her way out of the tub and towels herself urgently. Lightning flashes again and she squats into a ball, trying to remember: is this the *Reader's Digest* tip to survive lightning strikes, or is this how you fool grizzly bears? All she can recall is that you have to hit certain sharks flat on the nose. Her husband probably has read more carefully, but what does that mean? Did it ever mean anything? She realizes he has honed his skills for wholly improbable consequences, but flails at dangers easily averted. But is she any more agile? Better focused? When would she finally be prepared?

She crawls along the floor, patting the tile in search of the pink robe, which should radiate like a beacon. Impossibly, the robe isn't anywhere near the tub. She will have to wrap the towel like a sari. She moves close to the floor, orients herself, feels for hostile objects. The edge of the porcelain-or-not-porcelain tub. The sharp-cornered radiator. The inflexible door.

Lightning illuminates Beaker's terrified face in front of her, and she takes the dog by the collar. In his ear, she apologizes for all the terse walks he has endured lately, how she has yanked him past fire hydrants and fascinating trees. For this, too, she blames her husband. Beaker has been good to her, and Lila has been ungrateful, and now they will both die this way, huddled in terror, melted together by a lightning bolt into a mass of flesh and fur, a biological grilled cheese sandwich.

She pulls Beaker, who crouches too, alongside her to the bedroom. She can tell it's the bedroom by the carpet, which she generally won't touch with hand or vacuum. She feels her way to her husband's dresser, and with one hand on Beaker, she rifles through the drawers. No flashlight. A tornado siren sounds. She feels blindly for shoes that aren't high heels. She yelps with joy when her hand finds Birkenstocks. But they are her husband's Birkenstocks, large as canoe paddles. She gropes along the carpet until, thank heavens, Lila finds her own sandals and shoves her feet inside. The basement, she has to get to the basement: it is four stories down a rickety staircase, a place where it's rumored a woman was strangled in 1966. She reconsiders the weathermen's advice to seek interior rooms.

She finds her way to the doorknob where Beaker's leash hangs. She clamps it to his collar. The tornado sirens rise and fall, the cry of prehistoric beasts. Lila is unsure what to rescue from her home—long ago, it would have been wedding photos—

unsure where anything might be in this darkness, unsure how she'd juggle anything in her one free hand. Her husband is the carrier, the lifter, the one with the rebounder's reach. What is he doing in this storm? Should she care if he has a basement? She pulls Beaker with her into the pantry—her most interior room— and pulls the door. The towel slides to her feet. She locks the door as the rain pelts, the windows rattle and wheeze. She can't tell if she hears a roar like a locomotive.

She listens hard to the weather outside, perhaps inside, her apartment—it is now *her* apartment, for better or for worse. She tries to take comfort in a way to map and scale upheaval. Sifting the wreckage, the coroner might uncover an archeology of loneliness: a naked female body untouched by sex for at least a month. Twenty hand-cut pink felt penises. A cryptic note on glassware. A live dog in need of therapy. Picking over this sorry rubble, her mother wouldn't even know Lila had finally worn her gift. But perhaps, she thinks, as she finds enough hands to clutch Beaker tight, to pull the door and hold everything together in the howling dark, another story might be woven. A brighter thread could link the pieces scattered, even missing, in the wake: A Chagall wedding print on a pantry shelf, among faint and shriveling spices. A splendid—*splendid!*—candied robe. The grains of something once large and whole, evaporating into a wheel of light—an enormous sun, rising, shining, expansive in its warmth. One brilliant beam could catch a dragonfly. It could be as simple as that.

hold fast

Because he worries she might be drinking, Ted calls his daughter on Sunday night. The machine picks up and he begins to speak, awkwardly and with some reluctance, as he always does when he leaves messages. He doesn't trust digital technology and holds on to ancient, dependable appliances until they rattle apart. Unlike his daughters—Joanne, the older, steadier one, and Grace, who he is calling now—Ted believes in upkeep, repair, a code of ownership that seems to be falling out of fashion. It chafes him, the way people today can't be bothered with maintenance, let alone a wrench. They just buy and replace. Percolators, cars, televisions, spouses—anything can be left at the curb. Ted, who fixed vacuum cleaners until those, too, became cheap and disposable, refuses to take part in this new sensibility. He is loyal, though his wife Eloise used to laugh the nobility right out of that word. "Loyal?" she'd tease whenever he'd get self-righteous. "Try stubborn. You've been a codger since you were twenty."

He smiles, remembering Eloise, and loses track of what he is saying. Luckily, before things get too embarrassing, Grace picks up. "Hi, Daddy," she says, her voice raspy, like she's been asleep. Grace is thirty-eight but calls him her Daddy, and Ted is glad for it. Joanne started calling him Ted when she was a teenager, which feels wrong, even now.

He had raised his daughters as he thought a father should, with love and sternness, but at a safe distance from their daily dramas. He provided a full table and advice about practical matters, like buying bonds and dressing appropriately on airplanes. When he was young, Ted would tell them, men wore ties when they traveled and women wore stockings, sometimes gloves. Eloise tended to the details. She knew which boy Joanne liked, which girl was teasing Grace, and consulted him only at a crisis. But while Joanne outgrew the histrionics and is now a cheerful, married mother of two, Grace stayed edgy and dark. She is self-critical and grim and never wears make-up. Ted cannot quite read her.

Now, Grace clears her throat and asks, "How are you, Daddy?"

He replies, "Oh, fine." He refuses to itemize his aches and pains or discuss his digestion. But somehow, Grace understands sorrow and what it does to the body. So she asks, "How are you sleeping?" hitting the nail on the head.

"That's a good question," he answers. "Not so well, actually. On and off. A leaky faucet." Since he hit seventy, since Eloise passed, sleep has become elusive, unruly, overpowering. It seems absurd to have to work at it.

He asks about her job, and she tells him. At first, she seems all right. True, her diction is too precise and she speaks slowly, like he is losing his hearing (which he isn't), but there could be other reasons for this. For one, his daughter doesn't talk much. She is the curator of archives at a college library in Michigan. Ted thinks such a job can't be good for a young lady, all that hushed solitude and dim yellow lighting, the musty smell of bindings, things kept under glass.

He asks about her weekend and as she talks, some of her words stick together. She is clinging to consonants like toeholds, asking the same questions he's already answered. There is no question—Grace is drunk. What's worse, he believes that this is a pattern, one that organizes and explains some odd moments in the past. It explains why Eloise would hover when Grace came home to visit, why she inspected the trash afterwards, why Grace would turn in early but wake up late, unsteady and terse and puffy. It explains the urgent conversations that stopped whenever he walked in a room, the never-ending phone calls. Ted's throat tightens as he thinks of his wife, sitting alone on the couch long after he'd hung up the extension. What would she have said? In wondering this, he isn't sure if he means what she may have said to help out Grace, or what Eloise should have said to him.

For the time being, all he can do is keep Grace talking. But he's not good at it. He asks, "Heard from any of your friends lately?"

"Friends. That's a good one. Not too many left."

He tries again. "What about those girls you lived with back in college? The one with the suntan? Or that big fat smiley girl?"

She seems to think about it. "Well, Jennifer got married. You remember her, don't you?"

It takes awhile but in his mind, Jennifer becomes a meek girl with terrible teeth. "Right. So Jennifer finally settled down."

"Dad," Grace says, laughing sharply. "It was a nice ceremony. Everyone was very earnest. The band played oldies. You and mom would have cut a rug."

She is trying to be bright now, he can tell. He wonders if she got to dance, if anyone asked her. Grace has suffered some awful moments at dances. One Homecoming, her date up and left in the middle of the dance to go play basketball. The boy never told her he was leaving, never came back for her. Ted was dispatched to pick up Grace at the school, where he found her sitting outside on the steps—her hair just beginning to fall from its pins, her dress achingly pretty and crisp—ripping her corsage into smaller and smaller shreds.

Now he moves onto safer subjects. They talk for awhile about her latest decision: buying a new car. It has taken months for her to decide to buy, and she's hemming and hawing over models. But instead of getting irritated—he's the type who asks questions later—Ted looks forward to these conversations. He feels useful, sage. And he is getting out more, too. Every Friday, he walks to the corner bookstore to buy a new round of car magazines. In his erratic waking hours, he researches models, taking meticulous notes. He mails his reports to her from the post office across town, where the perky blonde at the counter calls him by name. "Good morning, Mr. Yates!" she'll say, right when he walks in, and he blushes as the folks in line turn and smile. Before his last trip to the post office, he ironed his collar and trouser pleats, though Eloise always did this for him, and it took awhile to get the hang of it. It surprised him, how much you could wrinkle with the best of intentions, how intricate, how careful Eloise's touch.

"But I like the Korean cars," Grace protests now in that peculiar starched voice. He gave the Korean cars one star in his last report.

"They crumple, honey. Besides, what do Koreans know about cars?"

"Daddy. It's a new century. Didn't you flip your calendar?"

"I've been researching them, Gracie. Old dad knows a few things."

"That's right. You do know things. You raised us well." She takes a deep, dramatic sigh he recognizes and dreads. "At least Joanne turned out well."

"Now Gracie," he says. With Grace, talk could turn at any moment, veer off into whines and wallows. He works to right the conversation. "You have lots of wonderful qualities. You help people. You're a smart, pretty girl."

"Ahh, that's right, my life is perfect. Starving people in China would kill for my life."

"Well, you do have it good."

Grace doesn't reply, and Ted hears her breathing. Then she asks, "What am I doing buying a car anyway?"

Ted says, "You need a car. Need to get out of that library and have some adventures."

He starts to tell her again about his first new Chevrolet, its taillights winking from fins, the rise of brand new highways, the dusty kick of back roads. Driving that big, smooth-handling car—Eloise beside him, her hair swirling in the breeze—he felt like something launched. A car would be the perfect way to get Grace moving, engaged in the world of living things. Who could be sulky with miles of road in the rearview and sunshine on the dash?

But Grace isn't listening. "Adventures," she says. "Ha. Who would go with me? Hercules?" Hercules is her dog, a quaking miniature greyhound.

"Well, no. But who needs a dog to drive to Colorado or California or—" he reaches, trying to remember the places she's mentioned, "or Maine?" He realizes he should have said Massachusetts. She's always talking about some bookish landmarks.

She sighs again and—this time he hears it—takes a drink. "But who do I have to see?" This is the sad voice that always asks why men are such jackasses.

"You can see all sorts of people," Ted says. "You can meet new people."

"There's a thought. Who?"

"I don't know. Other people taking trips."

"Oh, goody. I'm sure there are lots of nice men hanging around rest stops."

"That's not what I mean."

"It's all useless, Daddy. I make bad decisions."

"Now, Grace."

"What's the point, anyway."

"You need a car."

"Right. To make friends and influence people."

"Just to get out and see the world."

"Daddy. Please. Where in the world do I need to go?"

"You need to come and visit me."

He says it too fast, in a tiny old voice. Like that, he sounds like someone who gloms on to his children. He only wanted to get her head out of her own belly button, but now he's come off as grabby, like all his helping and researching has been a scheme for his benefit. It is unseemly. It isn't quite true.

Grace is quiet for a long moment.

"Honey?" he asks.

Finally, she says, "You're right, Daddy. I should just drive myself to Maine." With no trace of gumption. "I have to go."

"Grace."

"I'll call you next time, okay?" She hangs up. When he calls back, the line is engaged. It stays that way past midnight, past 4:30 in the morning, when Ted wakes up and tries again.

In over forty years of marriage, Ted thought there wasn't much left to know. He had assumed the secrets between him and Eloise were the ordinary kind: his occasional itch for the girl who helped at his shop, his constant wish for solitude, discreet loans to his gambling brother. Certainly nothing with consequence, like a drinking daughter or doctor visits. But Eloise withheld those things from him. She didn't tell him how sick she felt or how deeply Grace was troubled. Now, in the absence of his wife, everyday facts are splitting open into unpleasant mysteries.

He thinks of their last day at the house, how Eloise watched as he hung wash on the line. The young mother next door smiled and caught his eye, and he nodded, embarrassed to be fussing with underthings. Eloise had been tiring easily, he thought from a lingering flu, so she sat by in the shade by the impatiens, telling him his business. Putting him through the paces, almost as if she knew she would be leaving. They had just washed the windows, or more correctly, he had washed while she spotted the spots. Now her voice was high and sharp in a way that needled him. "Higher, Ted," she shouted as he pinned the sheets. "You don't want them to drag."

She could have told him anything then. That it was hard for her to breathe. That in her chest there were pockets of sickness, that he should be concerned. Then he could have told her the things you tell your wife when she's fading away.

But instead he rolled his eyes and fumbled with the clothespins. He kept her to his back. Before she passed out in the lawn chair, before he watched her heart beat on a tiny television screen, before their neighbor unpinned and folded the wash and left it on their doorstep, the only sound between Ted and his wife was the flapping of a sheet.

It's another thing to keep him up nights, that sound, the snap of a line pulled taut.

He has agreed to watch Joanne's children while she and her husband go off to Vegas, so Ted arrives on his daughter's doorstep with his small hard suitcase and favorite pillow. Not that the pillow will make a difference. All week, he has tried calling but Grace won't pick up. Now he is restless and tired and feeling hurt, whittled to a nub.

For the next week, all Ted can do during the days while the grandkids are in school is sit like a toadstool on Joanne's bright floral couch and watch the cable television. It doesn't help. The grandkids poke fun at his rabbit-eared RCA and say he is out of touch with reality, but it turns out that reality in all its screaming color can fast deplete a person. On cable, there are trials of children who kill their parents and skyscrapers collapsing into dust, and at two in the afternoon, you can watch, on several stations, animals of various species being born. Kittens in a crate, human babies in a tub, all making their slimy, squinched-up way into a world of lights and cameras. When his own children were born, Ted stayed in the waiting room and maintained what Eloise called his strong and silent act, even though inside, he quivered like an egg yolk. But he didn't get sappy like these fathers on cable. Times have certainly changed. Young people have gone completely crazy. Young women jiggle their bottoms like chimpanzees and fall out of bikinis. Young men are arrogant or queer. Teeth and hair and belly buttons all gleam with ornament. And everywhere, cameras go behind the scenes—or worse, under the skin. There are shows where people get fat sucked from their bodies with giant medical vacuums—if only he had applied himself, Ted thinks, amused and queasy, he could have been a millionaire. But who would have dreamed of using a vacuum for such a purpose? Who looked at a hose and a dimpled thigh and cried *Eureka?*

Even the actresses of his generation are unrecognizable, old starlets with faces stretched so tight they're practically looking out their ears. Nothing on cable resembles his life. Over the years, he felt a kinship with Dick Van Dyke; as whining teenagers, the girls called him "Archie Bunker." But there aren't any shows about old widowers with drinking daughters who don't answer the phone. Nothing illuminates Grace's gloom or reveals a way to lift it. Instead, on television, the elderly whisk grandchildren from swings in a haze of pain-free sunlight, or they collapse, alone, in heart attacks, or they sit like lumps as motorized lifts move them place to place. Old age is nothing but steady decline, requiring supplements. Not one old man on daytime television is capable of fixing a thing.

Fed up, he finds Joanne's Dirt Devil and strips it clean, right there on the living room rug. The tools feel right, move easily. Laying out each part, he could be ten again, fooling with his mother's Electrolux, its body sleek and silvery as a flying saucer, its whirling, star-shaped brush. The first time he took apart a machine, he was trying to solve a puzzle. Watching his grandma's stand-up Kenmore eat dirt, its two big headlights like alien eyes, he wanted to know, *Where does it all go? Show me,* he said, *Where does it go?* and his grandfather answered, *In its belly.* But Ted's grandfather told many lies, so Ted pulled the machine to pieces. His grandma strapped him when she walked in, seeing metal everywhere, those funny bug-eyes lying in the pile, lost and blind. She said she had saved a long time for that sweeper and Ted would damn well fix it. He was seven. But he did it, fine-tuning the intake port and speeding up the motor. Tinkering proved to be his first and only skill. He had terrible vision for far away objects, couldn't see a football until it hit him, and even with glasses, blackboard figures got jumbled in his head. But vacuums had parts that you could hold in your hand, pieces you could see. Put them together, they made a tangible whole, something that helped to keep a home.

He's thinking about this when the phone rings. The machine picks up and he hears Grace.

"Hey, Jo," she says. "It's my lunch hour and I'm calling to say hi. You're probably out doing interesting things. I'm just here in the stacks, collecting paper cuts."

Ted's knees creak as he stands up, and he stumbles over the Dirt Devil. He makes his way to the phone.

"Anyway, just wondering how you are. I'm okay, I guess. Missing Mom, you know, all that. Dad keeps calling and leaving these awful rambling messages. It's sad but making me sort of nuts. It's like he's stalking me."

Ted hesitates, wanting to make her stop, wanting to hear what she confides.

She says, "He wants me to visit, but God, what a thought. Can't you picture us, gaping like a couple of gutted fish, making small talk in that kitchen?"

Ted's heart sinks, and this dislodges a memory from the time Grace was a bitter teenager: Eloise, trying to cheer her up, saying, "Why don't you have one of your friends over? It might be nice to have a visitor." And Grace, miserable child, answering, "Oh, Mother. And make my friends suffer, too? Why would anyone want to be *here?*"

Now Grace says, "Anyway, call me, Jo. I'll be home tonight." The machine beeps.

Ted leans against the counter and plays the message back. Grace's voice is clear and sober, but that's cold comfort now. He is tempted never to call her again, this ungrateful, sullen daughter. He has spent all this time worrying, and for what? So she could call him names. But as he simmers down, he realizes there is a lot she isn't saying. He remembers how years ago, Eloise could have slapped their daughter when she ridiculed their house. And yet, Eloise didn't react at all, didn't even demand an apology. She just shook her head and said, "Grace lashes out when she's vulnerable, Ted. I don't think she has any friends to invite." What riled him, Eloise could see right through, hold up before him like a road map.

Scattered everywhere on the rug in front of him are the entrails of the vacuum. On television, a salesman opens the door to a Honda Accord. Four stars, Ted remembers. Reliable. It occurs to him that he should visit Grace, take a look up-close, for himself. She needs a good firm talking-to. Deciding this weighs on his bones, but at the same time, he feels charged. He will have to put the Dirt Devil together and plan the trip and take a nap before the grandkids rush home. First, he deletes Grace's message—the push of a button, every bit of it, gone.

Opening the door, taking his coat and umbrella, Grace is animated, hostessy, a person not at all his daughter. She is wearing ruby-red lipstick and a mannish turtleneck and a long, black witchy skirt, and she looks heavier around her chin and hips, older, more severe. It's bewildering to see her primped like this, colorful and smiling, her hair swept into a librarian's bun, stuck through with shiny chopsticks. Clearly, she's been warned of his arrival— Joanne's eyes widened, alarmed, when he told her—but Ted expected that. Driving up, he thought of that jungle show, *Wild Kingdom,* where they set up cameras in the brush to capture lions hunting and nursing their cubs, all in their natural habitat. He realized that's what he is hoping to do: see Grace in her natural habitat. It would be harder, of course, for him to blend in and observe, especially here in her weird, stark home. The bathroom door is painted purple, hanging over it, a gargoyle.

Harder to handle is Grace's good cheer. "Well, isn't this a lovely surprise!" she says. "I'm so glad you've come to visit!" She claps her hands like Betty Furness opening the door to a Westinghouse.

"Same here," Ted says. To show he means it, he pats her on the shoulder. And truly, he is happy to see her; his heart feels fluttery, light. He last saw her at Christmas, their first since Eloise passed. They look at each other with tight, expectant smiles.

"Gosh, when was the last time you were here, Daddy?" she asks. "It must have been when I first moved."

She deposits his suitcase in the den, a shadowy room that smells like bleach. When she moved in, Ted thought her apartment was bleak, in need of Eloise's embroidered touch, but he soon realized its dark wood floors and heavy doors held a sunlessness that suited Grace. There's something different about it now. It is shiny. Every surface gleams with effort: the veneer of settling doubts.

Ted asks, "How is this beast?"

Hercules minces up and licks Ted's hand, and Ted allows this. If fragility could take a shape, it would be this teacup of a dog. Grace smiles and calls the dog, who walks everywhere on tiptoe. Hercules follows them into the living room and nibbles a squeaking rubber turtle.

Ted and Grace sit on hard-backed chairs. Ted looks around. The walls are the color of Grace's lipstick and decorated with paintings of fruit in bowls. The single painting of a human being is of a glowing white, naked, bleeding man draped, dead, over the edge of a bathtub. No wonder his daughter dissolves into drink each night, he thinks, in this room without so much as a cushion.

"I would have cleaned if I'd known you were coming," Grace says, when obviously, she's scrubbed all morning. "The place is such a mess."

"Gracie, please. The place looks fine. Your mom would have liked that statue." He points to a bust of a strapping male torso, its genitals exposed.

She flushes and laughs too hard. "See what I mean? I'm not used to visitors."

"Oh now, I'm not company. I'm family."

There is a long moment where they don't say anything. Then Grace remembers to ask about Ted's drive, which was rainy and harrowing. His tiny Dodge was constantly nudged by trucks. He doesn't tell her that he confused her street name with one from his childhood and exited the interstate early, how he drove, lost, for nearly thirty minutes before he realized his mistake.

Grace is talking about her schedule. "And I don't know if I can take a day off, so I'm not sure what you had in mind to do."

"Don't fret about me," Ted says. "I'll just putter. Need anything fixed?"

Grace's smile looks ready to crack. "Well, I'll have to think about it. Just how long did you plan to stay?"

Ted can see what she's thinking: her father nosing through closets, ferreting beneath the countertops. And who can blame her? He remembers how the girls used to mess with every brush and fan blade in his workshop until he installed a lock. Drove him crazy, little hands on his screwdrivers, turning washers into earrings for dolls.

She says, "Because I have some deadlines and maybe some meetings and I don't want to bore you all the time."

Ted sees that his daughter is puffing her feathers, making a show of good intentions. Her hostess act is really plumage—resplendent, distracting, big and grand, keeping him at bay. If he wants to fade into the woodwork and see the real Grace, he will have to smooth her ruffles. But how? As she offers him pillows and snacks and ice water, and he declines, Ted realizes two things: one, that Grace thinks she is being charitable, doing her duty, by keeping her old man company. And two, that his daughter's better, kinder instincts might be used to his advantage.

So he says, in a small voice, "I know you're busy, honey. I won't be trouble. It's just quiet at home, by myself. Tough-going without your Mom."

She stops her list of things to do. Her face takes on the look of eight-year old Gracie, finding a stray cat.

He sighs. "Guess I got so caught up missing her, I forgot about your schedule. But don't you worry, I can go as soon as I rest up from the drive."

That's all it takes. "Oh Daddy," she says, rising, giving him a quick hug. "It's no trouble at all. I'm glad you're here. Really. I'll make time. I mean, the things I work with are centuries old—what's a few more days?"

For the rest of the evening, as they share a soggy lasagna she has baked and talk about dying relatives, Grace still burns a little bright, though at a lower wattage. He notices two bottles of wine by the sugar jar, which she makes a point of ignoring. There is almost nothing in her refrigerator: ketchup, Pepsi, gourmet dog food. Before turning in, she gives elaborate instructions for using the shower, and Ted observes the leaking spigot, the wobbly curtain rod: ways he can simplify her life. With these hardwood floors, he is sure she doesn't own a vacuum. But between walking Hercules tomorrow while she is at work and poking around and tightening screws, there will be plenty for him to do.

That night, Ted dreams he is pushing baby Grace in her stroller, Eloise by his side, down the long steep street where he once lined up his brother's aggies and watched them roll downhill. It is late afternoon and the moon is high and he points it out to Eloise, but when he turns, he realizes she is gone. Grace's stroller makes a sudden squeak. One wheel starts wobbling, then another, and then the handles slip away. The stroller races down the sidewalk, squeaking, squeaking, out of reach, and he runs to catch it before Grace is thrown into the street. Traffic whips by and the stroller is squeaking and he leaps and grabs and misses. Squeaking, squeaking, the stroller rolls and teeters to a stop. Finally, Ted can breathe. That is when he sees the truck bearing down on her, too fast for him to move. He wakes up, stunned to find himself on a black leather couch in a blood-red room, sun under the shade, a dog in the corner chewing on what looks like a little rubber turtle.

He bangs his knee against the table and his back throbs from the drive, and he walks around in a cloud all day, rooting through Grace's cupboards for oatmeal, picking out the raisins. He walks Hercules to the corner, where a group of teenagers shouts things like "Yo Cujo!" and "Grrr!" until he crosses the street, and he is too caught up in the leash to grab a newspaper before the machine door slams. After tinkering with the shower, he sits and waits. His urgency is fading; it's difficult to fix someone's life when nothing is apparently broken.

Then Grace comes home restless, unwilling to sit or cook, and she suggests they go out. She takes him to a museum on campus where they stare at paint spatters and pornography. He can't make sense of art, it seems—lip prints on a toilet seat, jars of blood or urine or worse. He grunts whenever she tries to explain some jumbled mess she seems to like. His feet grow tired. Later, she drives his car around the city and points out dull attractions, acting like the Grace he knows and will never understand. "To your right, it's the Country Kitchen buffet. Ooh look, tonight's special is yams," she says. After dinner at a foo-foo restaurant— curly salads and runty steaks and mashed potatoes in swirls, like icing—they drive by a long line of adolescents with shockingly colored hair. Grace laughs, and in her tour guide voice says, "Now on your left, it's the undergraduates lining up at a local club for their nightly ritual of thrashing, copulating, and puking." Ted doesn't know what stuns him more: the children, or how she puts it.

The next day, with his digestive tract in a tangle from dinner and Grace taking the day off, they go to a movie, and Ted is just happy to be somewhere not eating, not talking, and not walking through her dirty neighborhood. She chooses a thriller set in Alaska, where the sun apparently doesn't set, and it is a good movie although Grace complains about lots of things he hadn't noticed.

"Leave it to Hollywood," she says as they walk out into day- light. "I mean, are we really supposed to believe Hilary Swank would just wander into that cabin?"

"You talking about that girl cop?" Ted asks.

She says, "Yes, Daddy. The 'girl cop.' The boy cop is the one that saves her." Lighting a cigarette—has she always smoked?— she adds, "But who's surprised by that."

That night, they have spicy, ethnic take-out food and run out of things to talk about. Grace makes faces as she sips her ice water (she says it tastes like rust) and sits on the balcony, smoking, and constantly taps her large, unfeminine feet. They bump elbows in the hallway and open doors into one another's faces. The radiator clanks out heat. Throughout the evening, each of them steps on Hercules, who yelps and wags his slender tail. Apologizing.

By the middle of the week, nothing is getting accomplished. Without his noticing exactly how, he sees the wine on the counter has vanished. He thinks she sneaks it on the fire escape, or pours it in her thermos. It's clear that he is losing time. Now they're about as far apart as poles on an electric motor: north and south. They need a project, a common goal to spin between them like a rotor. He decides they should go to a car dealership, and this is where things take a downturn. Later, he realizes he must have expected some grand adventure: a salesman greeting them, presenting car after shining car like a Busby Berkeley musical; Grace delighting in the one she would buy; Ted approving; and a current passing between them, the way it did when Ted gave her Eloise's photo albums for Christmas.

But what actually happens is quite annoying. The salesman is pushy, and from the start, Grace despises him.

"Now at our dealership, we customize each vehicle. It's a mandatory package," the salesman, Darius, says.

"And a mandatory kickback for you guys," Grace says, folding her arms.

"Well," says Darius, smiling at Ted, who must seem, in comparison, downright affable. "We provide wheel locks and mud flaps and undercoating for half the retail price."

"Right," Grace says. "Because you care so much about my needs, you're willing to make the sacrifice."

"Grace," Ted interrupts. "You live in Ann Arbor. Undercoating is important."

"Daddy," she says. "It's nothing but money in their pocket. Cha-ching! Right, Darius?"

The salesman looks at Ted, imploring, but the matter is out of his hands. He doesn't know what, if anything, will satisfy his daughter. As they walk the lot, Grace nay-says sticker prices, colors, highway mileages. She guffaws and snorts. Ted imagines his research, his notes carefully folded in envelopes, fluttering piece by piece into the sky.

After an hour, Darius shrugs. "It sounds like you've made up your mind," he says, handing Ted his card. "Sir, don't hesitate to call if you're ever interested for yourself."

By the time they leave, Ted is ready to blow a gasket. All he wants is untroubled sleep and bland soup from a can. But Grace insists they stop for dinner at a place near her apartment. It is a dark little joint that's more Ted's speed, where a hamburger is called a hamburger. Grace makes a production of greeting the hostess by name, waving broadly to the bartender. "I'm a regular," she announces, with all the pride of being in a place where people should recognize you.

And here, for the first time since he has been keeping watch, Ted sees Grace drink. She starts with a glass of merlot. He is so worn out from bickering and coaxing and walking around, he can't help but order a beer. As it happens, this is a bad idea, since it seems to give Grace a kind of springboard. After their appetizers, she orders another merlot; with dinner, another still; a slight lift of her finger, a nod and smile, and glass after glass appears. All the while, she gets looser, more chatty with the waiter, a polite young man with an earring in his nose.

"Steve, Steve, you're always so good to me," she says.

The boy raises an eyebrow. "You've been here before, ma'am?"

Grace flushes and looks at Ted. "Steve, my man. You served me last week."

Steve smiles vacantly and holds the tray to his chest.

"Grace Yates," she says slowly, like he's a foreigner. "Cheeseburger, merlot, sometimes pie? Corner booth with the good light for reading? I'm always reading. I've seen you when you get off work—I walk my little greyhound."

Steve lights up. "Oh! That funny dog! I didn't realize that was you." They both laugh and then it's quiet; what more can they say?

Steve takes their plates and, no dummy about tips, makes an effort to call Grace "Miss Yates." But as he and Grace work through pieces of pie, Ted feels embarrassed. It's the same feeling as when he picked her up from the Homecoming dance after her date abandoned her, the feeling he's had whenever he's seen her alone and vulnerable in public. He remembers her awkward stab at musicals when she was in high school, how his breath caught when he saw her in the spotlight, hoping she'd be transformed. But she was just Grace, a gawky kid in a bright pink halter top, a beat behind the music, leaden and pale beside her castmates, her lips moving instead of smiling. "She's counting, Ted," Eloise whispered as they sat in the crowd. "Oh, dear. Just like her father." By this, Eloise meant Grace was hopelessly earthbound, utterly deliberate in all things. Ted felt her pain. He had, in fact, met Eloise because of such traits. Running his business from his neighbor's garage, he finally saved enough to buy a good suit, which meant he could go to a YMCA social and find a girl he could, perhaps, marry. He was twenty-five and moving past the decent age of courtship. But he'd never danced at a function before, never danced much at all, and almost couldn't form the words to ask anyone to two-step. It took Eloise, so much younger and bolder, to grab his hand and drag him to the floor, where he, like a doofus, stared at his feet and counted until she crouched into his sightline. "Lose something?" she asked, laughing, when the situation was quite the opposite. He had found her. Her dimples, lopsided, disarmed him.

But their daughter has no one to soften her edges, he realizes, watching her clean her plate. Her emptiness fills him with aching. How often does she go unnoticed, he wonders, or hope to catch someone's eye? She raises her finger and before he knows it, Ted is reaching out.

"No, Grace. You can't keep doing this. You need to stop. That's enough for tonight."

She shakes his hand off like it's dirty. "For God's sake, Daddy. I'm getting the check."

He folds his hands on the table like a child. She glares at him. Something sharp and steely is aimed directly at his heart.

"Sorry," he says. "Thought you were having another."

"Pie?" she asks. "Gosh, Daddy, you're a watchdog."

But they both know what he means. She counts out cash and hands Steve the bill. "See you next time, Miss Yates," he grins. She puts her billfold in her pocketbook, looks ready to stand, to go.

Ted feels the moment slipping. He needs to say something wise and fatherly to fix the mess she's in. So he tells Grace she is heading for danger, that her mother would hate to see her like this. He describes the many times he could have thrown in the towel but soldiered on. He never once felt sorry for himself. He starts off stern but words begin escaping, out of order, in a rush. He tells her he might have built walls and he's sorry for that, sorry if she felt shut out. She has to understand, things were different for him. His parents were farmers, salt of the earth. He only saw them smile once, on his wedding day. What a day that was, Eloise laughing all through the ceremony. But his point was getting away, what was it? That she shouldn't think everyone else was perfect. Joanne has problems—she yells at her kids, who never do chores, and her husband is a lunkhead. Everyone has problems, he says, even him. And that's his point. The point is he found ways to handle things, like planning his parents' funeral, or that awful time he had to identify his brother's body, beaten to a pulp by thugs. It hurt like hell when business fell off and he had to close up shop. And it was almost unbearable, listening to doctors apologize for fixes that didn't work. Almost unbearable, holding fast to Eloise's hand, her small pretty hand, as it grew cool.

By the time he stops talking his eyes are wet and his nose is runny. Grace slides him a napkin. He blows his nose in a honk. People look, then look away. He is shot through with a kind of trembling. Everything inside him feels loose and wobbly. He is afraid to open his mouth, what might rattle out.

"Ready to go, Daddy?" his daughter asks. Her voice is kind. She catches his eye but then, for his sake, busies herself with the zipper on her purse.

He nods, trying to focus. So many thoughts flickering by. He hasn't been the least bit instructive, hasn't said one sensible thing, and soon he will leave here just as he came, make his way back to an empty house. He stands and takes his coat from the rack by their booth, concentrating on its buttons. Like a tap on the shoulder he hears a voice, a child's voice, like his grandson's. *Show me,* the voice is saying. He looks around but no one is talking to him. *No fooling this time,* the voice says. *Show me. Where does it all go?* But before he can answer, Grace takes his arm, and they brace each other for the walk.